I0629827

LAND

OF

ARLENM

SAMANTHA GOLLAKNER

To all of my guides, both physically and spiritually.

Thank you.

CHAPTER ONE:

The darkness that engulfs the mortals becomes thicker with every second that ticks past. I can hear Austin's rough panting from here.

Suddenly, a bright, white light casts down around them, basking my mortals in a sea of false illumination.

A man walks out of the shadows, forcing all of their attention onto him.

It does not take me long to understand why his presence feels so familiar to me.

Of course! It is Master Brutus! Who else would kidnap me, transport me back to my world in a capsule of humiliation and then send my own game pieces on a rapid, man-hunt to come rescue me?

My hatred for him burns deeper by the moment.

Master Brutus allows his head to fall in a side to side, sweeping manner as he scans each of my pawns.

He allows his voice to travel in a gentle sway, "Welcome to world eight. I would say that it is a pleasure to see all of you here. Unfortunately, that would be a lie and I cannot stand anything more in this universe than deceitful people."

A small pause finds itself entangled in his throat as he becomes lost in his own trail of thoughts.

Master Brutus quickly clears his mind, "Now, your next

mission is simple. Go save Arlenm. There is no time limit in this realm. It is the most difficult challenge you have faced yet. Anyone can conquer someone else, but not everyone can defeat themselves. The Elders and I have taken that into consideration and we have decided to give you a break. That is our gift to you for this world. Also, I would like you all to remember, every destination has a journey to get there. Please, try to survive yours."

Master Brutus pushes his weight into a backwards movement while spinning his figure to the left.

He raises his right hand to rest beside his head, snapping his fingers sharply before disappearing into the unknown.

Austin's attention shifts onto the gentle pulsing beneath his feet.

His head whips in a fast motion towards Luke and Emily, "Do you feel that?"

They both silently nod their heads in agreement.

Emily parts her lips slightly, wanting to find her voice, but it becomes stolen as the floor opens beneath their soles. This action caused by Master Brutus, throws them into a deep, black void.

I watch from miles away. I feel completely helpless as their blackened figures fling their arms and legs in a frantic attempt to grab hold of something stable.

The fading scream of my last remaining, female pawn sends a shot of fear to run in an upwards motion along both sides of my spine.

CHAPTER TWO:

Austin is the first one to connect with something solid. The front half of his body slams into a damp, wooden surface.

I watch Luke and Emily come tumbling into view moments after.

Austin rolls the weight of his head to the right, taking a moment to enjoy the cool flush of the surface below him that is now brushing against his sensitive skin.

He squints his eyes sharply. The muscles lining his upper-back strain as he hoists himself onto the unbalanced platform of his kneecaps.

The weight of his head scans the area around him in a fast sweep from the left to the right. He finds that they are currently in some form of a tunnel, constructed out of roaring waves of water.

The sound of the molecules spinning around them bounces against the inside of his mind as he continues to get a firm grip on the new surroundings.

His search has given him the information that they are on some type of a rather large ship. They are currently positioned in the vacant rear.

Austin inhales a deep breath in through his nose, the harsh scent of sea life engulfs his senses.

The reflective surface of his vision informs me that he is currently staring at a ten-foot-tall by twenty-foot-tall beam that is stationed roughly six-feet away from him.

It is holding up one of the sun beaten, white sails.

Austin's face strains as he pulls himself up into a full stance, walking towards the pole.

He allows the grooved pads of his right fingertips to brush against the dark brown, soggy wood.

His eyes sweep along the flooring beneath him. His mind reels at the flaking, sea foam green paint.

Drops of water splash up from the mass of hydration around them. The beads land against the cracked surface of Austin's lips. The familiar sensation of salt runs across his taste buds.

Emily shatters his daydream-like state by speaking in a choking whisper, "What are we going to do first?"

Austin's eyes widen sharply, "Luke, what do you think we should do?"

Luke steps forward slightly, "I think that our best option is to explore the ship."

Austin clears his throat roughly, waving the structure of his left arm away from his body, "After you."

Luke cannot help but to release an already fading grin, "My pleasure."

CHAPTER THREE:

Emily mindlessly trails in silence as her thoughts carry her to a question, "Do either of you have any idea why we are on this boat or why they couldn't just magically poof us there?"

A small laugh creeps up the back of Luke's throat, "That would be too easy. We are supposed to be learning along the way. Do not be so disheartened about this little detour. Enjoy the journey."

Austin sighs gently, beginning to feel the intensity of anxiety regaining control over his thoughts and actions.

He finds that his mind is now running at one-hundred miles per hour. The gentle pound of his heart can be felt by the inner confines of his ears. The interior lining of his hands leak sweat as every step taken by his restless legs leads him closer to his fear of the unknown.

The chaos inside of him is brought to a sudden halt as the waves guiding the boat forward begin to become extremely choppy.

It sends my mortals sailing towards the front of the boat in a mixture of flailing limbs as they are frantically attempting to readjust their postures.

Austin strains his voice, "What happened?"

Luke shakes his head slowly, not taking his eyes off of the direction that they are heading, "We have to be really careful of our thoughts in this world. Our thoughts control the journey. If our thoughts emit positive vibrations then the water will remain calm. However, at the slightest hint of negative energy, the currents will become enraged. The more you feed the emotion, the more intense the journey becomes."

Emily begins to pick up speed from the back of the group, extending her right arm between their shoulders, "What is that?"

Luke squints his vision sharply in the detailed direction, "That is where the crew is."

Austin's eyes widen in shock at what he is hearing, "Are we sure that we want to go that way?"

Luke nods once in a firm manner, speaking in a calm tone, "Yes. We have done nothing wrong. What should we be fearful of? We were dropped here against our will into this world. It is only polite that we go say hello and introduce ourselves."

Austin can feel the sparks of fear burning the back of his throat as his feet mindlessly carry him onwards.

Luke leads the other two mortals into a small, dark brown, wooden frame with a matching door panel that was just left cracked open.

Luke allows his right foot into the chamber first. He ducks his head slightly to avoid a collision.

His eyes widen when he sees the first creature they have found on this plane. Now, standing three-feet in front of them. The creature is unknowing of their presence, yet carelessly controlling the vessel.

Luke's bottom lip drops slightly as he takes one stride closer trying to examine the creature's form.

Luke admires the cream colored, slip-on shoes resting along the Captain's feet as well as the relaxed, gray pants that hang against her waist. A beige, knitted sweater covers her torso with the sleeves rolled three-fourths of the way up her arm to reveal the ink embedded into her skin underneath.

The Captain appears to be in her early twenties. Loose strands of light brown hair are held in a messy bun atop of her head. Not a single difference can be found from the water's hue to the glowing shade of her blue eyes.

My pawns begin to feel peace in the moment while they continue to try and read the Captain's energy.

Luke takes a single stride further in a forward manner.

The sound of his soles hitting the wooden surface causes the Captain's head to lean in Luke's direction.

A calm vibration is released from her throat, "Hello. It is nice to see a familiar face."

Luke tilts his head to the right, "Do you know me?"

The Captain steps forward, extending her open, right hand, "No, not on this plane. I just have not seen another human in so long, I was captivated by your presence. I apologize for the misunderstanding. My name is Sam."

Luke extends his open, right palm away from his form in a horizontal movement as a sign of peace, "I am Luke. This is Emily and Austin. We have been made passengers of your boat against our will. We would like permission to ride your transportation system."

He pauses briefly, leaning the front half of his body towards her, speaking in a soft whisper, "How did you get here? Did Arlenm kidnap you, too?"

A growing smile leaks against her lips, "Yes, you may stay on board the ship as long as you need. No, I was not kidnapped. I was lost, I came here to find my way home."

Luke nods quickly in her direction, "Thank you."

The Captain gently drops her head to the right, staring out into the waves, "You might want to be cautious of this frequency. Things can get pretty intense around here. Some of the people from the outer world might try to kidnap you in your sleep. I am not trying to frighten you and I know, it sounds strange I am sure, but it is something that has happened before. There are some guests on the boat, we call them by different names. They enjoy stealing energy. Watch out for them, they already saw you."

Luke tries to speak in a strong tone, only the words stumble across his tongue, "Should we be concerned?"

She does not allow her energy to lower in spite of his negative vibration, "There is no reason to panic, Luke. If it will make you feel any better, I can have some of my most trusted friends escort you to your rooms."

Luke can only move his head in a forward manner of approval.

CHAPTER FOUR:

The Captain smiles at my mortals with a relaxed grin, "I really want you guys to meet the rest of my crew. I want them to show you to your rooms for a few reasons. One of those reasons is so that you can rest. You must be exhausted after your journey this far."

The Captain hears a new noise entering the threshold.

She lifts her open, right palm in a vertical motion, "Great! You are here!"

The pawns turn around to see what has caused such a shift in her.

Emily's eyes reflect the image of a man, who stands nearly six-feet in height. His outer layer is two different components swirling together. One belongs to human flesh, the other mimics that of a soft, red coral. Pieces of the sea creature are sticking out of his head. The same replication is sprouting from his hands in place of where his fingers should be.

Luke tilts his head in a smooth, backwards motion towards the Captain, "Who is he?"

The Captain laughs gently, "He is part of the crew. There are four of us who run the ship. I am sure you will meet the others along the way."

Luke smirks at the new member of the room while directing his words towards the Captain, "What is his name?"

She shifts her attention to drape over the man with pride, "Kave."

Kave perks his head up at the acknowledgement of his title, "Yes?"

The Captain scans his figure in a fast glance, "Please, help them towards the sleeping chambers."

Kave nods his head once in a slow manner. He does not utter a single sound as he turns his direction to head out of the Captain's quarters and onto the deck.

Luke pushes his weight in a forward motion, silently informing the others that it is time for a change of scenery.

Emily allows a fast yawn to slip out of her lips.

Kave turns his head over his left shoulder towards her, "You will be able to rest soon."

She finds that her attention is being shifted off of Kave and onto the vast unknown of this world surrounding them.

The amazement she is feeling seems to have given her a miniature, second wind.

Her admiration can be seen through the glossy surface of her vision, "Luke, what do you think is out there, beyond this tunnel of water?"

Before Luke has a chance to answer, their attention becomes shot in a forward manner towards Kave.

He speaks quickly, "Trust me, you do not want to go out

there."

Luke tunes out their conversation, focusing on the flight of metal stairs they are about to descend.

At this current moment, they are unable to see anything but darkness.

CHAPTER FIVE:

Luke ducks his head slightly, advancing into the black hole.

Kave strikes the end of a match against the frame, igniting a lantern that he picked up along the journey.

Something in the distance has captured Austin's interest.

He shakes his head in a side-to-side motion, "Luke, do you see that up there?"

I cannot help but notice that both Emily and Luke begin tossing their heads in different directions trying to find what he is seeing.

Both of them come up empty for an answer.

Austin can see the confusion melting from their vision.

Urgency runs through his extended, right, index finger which is pointed ahead of them, "Up there. Do you see it? The green eyes."

Luke squints his vision, leaning the upper portion of his body forward.

He tilts his head towards Kave, "Who is that up ahead?"

Kave does not allow even his vision to shift under the question.

He makes sure to respond in a calm tone, "That is Kemper. He is a friend. Another part of the crew."

The mortals turn their full focus back onto the stairwell just in time to find that the flickering flare of the flame is bouncing against a creature.

Everyone stops upon his entrance into the moment.

I notice that my humans cannot help but to admire him.

His figure, like the rest of the creatures here so far, resembles a lot of features that are human. His bright green eyes look even more alive now that we are able to see his olive shaded skin. Long strands of seaweed entangle themselves with his skin from his upper, right shoulder traveling in a downwards angle towards his waistline before tapering off down the side of his left leg.

Kave nods to him softly, "Kemper, these are the new guests for the trip. Captain told me to keep them comfortable."

Kemper kindly smiles in the direction of my earthlings, before tilting his focus onto Kave, "I must be going now. The captain called us up to the deck."

The humans follow his movements as he passes trying to get one, final glimpse of him before he disappears into the darkness.

Kave breaks their focus as a line of letters drain from his mouth, "Ah! I was wondering if we were going to run into you. There are some people that I would like you to meet."

Luke turns his attention back around to find that two, male shadows are now casting against the left wall.

Kave feels a slight smile creeping against his face as he turns towards my pawns, "People of Earth, I would like you to meet the rest of my crew. This is Outo."

Luke finds himself scanning the creature in a fast, vertical sweep. Strands of his short, black hair lay in a messy manner. A purple hue lines the inside of his eyes. Most of his figure mimics that of an Earth inhabitant, but a swirl of light gray, silky flesh travels down his form. Tiny, blush colored suction cups cover the inner belly of the eight arms that are distributed down both sides of his torso.

Outo flashes the humans a fast, half grin before Kave clears his throat, "And, this is Joxi."

Austin leans all of his weight onto his right leg allowing him to get a better look around Emily.

A tiger-like pattern of pink flesh runs over the pale skin around it. The creature bears small, black, soulless eyes and he has not broken the same, cheeky smile since he approached the group.

Kave releases a deep breath intertwined with disappointment, "Well, I better let you go. I know she only asks for assistance in times of major importance."

It does not take much convincing to get them moving in the right direction once more.

The rays of light shining off of the candle, burn against the surface of a large, locking wheel that is being used as a door handle.

Kave uses all of his weight and strength to push the sphere to the left, freeing the latch from the frame, "Come on. Your rooms are just up ahead."

They continue to advance through the entryway with uncertainty lined in every stride.

Their eyes are immediately affected by the lights after being in the dark for so long.

Austin can still taste the minerals along his tongue. He tries to remove the scent lingering in his nasal canals, that he collected while inside of the damp stairwell.

Emily begins looking around the area to find that they are currently standing in one of the halls on the ship, but it is completely empty.

Austin picks up on the vacancy as well, "Where is everyone else?"

Kave does not want to remain stagnant to that spot any longer, he turns sharply to the right without saying a word.

The humans stumble over their feet as they take off after him.

Kave speaks in a soothing manner, "Everyone is asleep. This is the normal sleeping hours for our world. I do not know how long you are going to be here, but I do suggest that you at least try to get used to it."

He refrains from talking momentarily, raising his right, index finger in a sweeping motion across the hall starting from the right, "Austin, you have the one on this side. Luke and Emily, you guys are going to be just across the hall to the left in room one-hundred and eight. Get some rest, we can speak more whenever you would like. You know where to find us in case you need anything. I hope you have a nice night."

CHAPTER SIX:

My mortals are awoken by some chaos in the hallway.

Austin stumbles in a half-dazed state towards the door to find Emily and Luke's heads poking into the excitement as well.

Emily looks across the space towards Austin, "I wonder what is going on?"

Luke tilts his head in a backwards pull, over his left shoulder to look at the clock, "Before we went to sleep. I was reading one of the pamphlets that said dinner was around this time. Do you guys want to go eat?"

Emily can feel the shock running against her words, "Dinner? How long were we asleep?"

Luke squints his right eye as he thinks, "About twelve hours."

Emily nods her head once while touching the surface of her stomach with her right palm, "Yes. I am starving."

Austin agrees, stepping fully out into the hall, shutting the door behind them.

The walk to the dining area takes no time at all to achieve.

Luke leads the pack into the propped open, double paneled, glass doors that construct the only entrance.

He is greeted by the hostess, who is stationed roughly three-feet away, behind a dark stained, wooden podium.

Austin finds himself captivated by the hostess. She stands roughly five-feet, four-inches tall. She has long, wavy, light brown hair that barely brushes against her shoulder blades. Her eyes match his for intensity, intertwined in the brightest of blue hues. Her pale skin appears cold under the warming radiance of color that is being emitted from areas of her figure that are covered in different shards of sea glass. The pieces range in color from blue, green, yellow, orange and red.

She notices them stall in the entryway, "Good evening. Welcome in. Is it just going to be the three of you tonight?"

Luke nods once, "Yes."

She does not allow her smile to fade an inch, "Great. Do you have a name for the reservation?"

Luke tilts his head to the right slightly, "A name?"

She pushes her point, this time with a firmer tone, "Yes. I need to know your name to be able to pull your table up on our system."

A soft grin rises to the left side of Luke's lips, "Master Brutus."

They watch in silence as the creature fumbles through a stack of note card size papers, "Of course, right this way, Mr. Brutus."

Luke nods once in a confident manner, following each one of her steps.

They currently see nothing, but a fourteen-foot, dark, wood panel for a wall to the left and the bathrooms appear to be stationed on their right.

The hostess makes a sharp, left turn.

Their eyes ignite with amazement as they look around the new area they just ventured into.

A glass wall is now positioned to their right which allows the guests a chance to see their food being prepared.

They try to keep their minds centered on the task at hand, trailing this woman. She leads them out onto the main floor. Nineteen tables are placed in a circle around a large, rectangular stage in the center of the room that is currently releasing puffs of fog from the nozzles that are placed around the perimeter.

The hostess finally stops progressing next to a table on the left side of the room, right in front of a stage.

The humans begin to make themselves feel at home as they all sit down around the table.

The hostess leans in slightly, "Your food and drinks will be out here shortly. Please, enjoy the show."

Luke raises his right hand sharply, waving it in a small motion in hopes of snatching her attention.

He whispers in a harsh manner, hoping he does not disturb the other guests, "Wait! We did not order anything yet."

She releases a soft laugh, "We do not have a menu here. So, what you get was specifically picked by the Chef, just for you. He basis this decision off of how he felt when he saw you walk in."

Luke pushes his mouth into a forced frown of amusement.

The next thing he knows, he feels his focus drop towards his left, where a vine is handing him his plate. To his right, another piece of stringed foliage is providing him with a beverage.

Luke looks down into the cream-colored mug crafted from clay. Inside is a steaming hot, light caramel colored fluid with jasmine petals infused throughout the droplets.

Luke licks his lips at the thought of the drink, but first he wants to give it a moment to cool off.

He leans his head in a downwards movement to see that two cabbage and carrot wraps line the food carrier with a thick, creamy, pink dipping sauce made from the nature of this realm.

Luke tilts his head towards Austin's items. His plate is smothered with seaweed wrapped, cream cheese sticks and a spicy dipping sauce topped off with a bowl of turnip soup.

Austin raises his mug towards his lips, inhaling a small sip of his drink. A wilted, lavender petal becomes stuck against the upper-half of his mouth.

Austin turns his vision towards Emily's food to examine her meal.

She was given a bowl that is constructed out of lettuce. Inside it is filled with wild rice, black beans and a heaping mound of fried onion straws that are drizzled with a creamy sauce to finish it off.

However, much like Austin, her focus is solely on getting something to quench her dry throat.

A wave of daisy washes along her taste buds, slowly creeping across the other platforms of her senses as well.

It does not take them long to scarf down their entire meal.

It feels to me as though we have only been here for a few moments.

They are pleased to find that their dinner has already been taken care of, thanks to Master Brutus.

I notice that Luke places his palms against the edge of the table, to aid himself into a vertical placement.

However, he does not make it far, stopping halfway due to something that catches his attention out of the corner of his vision.

He turns his head towards the stage, where a large cylinder of golden light drains down from the ceiling towards the elevated platform in the center of the restaurant.

Luke slowly begins lowering himself back into a sitting placement.

His pupils dart along the skirting of the area to see that all the staff are now bowing down in response to this light source.

Luke becomes intrigued by this and can feel a deep itch tearing him apart in desperation to know more.

At this point, all of my mortals have turned their attention into the frequency of the holographic image being pieced together in front of them.

It is a man, who looks to be around his mid-to-late twenties in the measurement of human years.

He has messy, brown hair that pulls the color out of his calming, blue eyes dulling them to a dim glimmer of hope.

A good-sized fin is protruding out from the center of his spine, it extends roughly a foot from his figure. The majority of his form is cloaked in the smooth, gray flesh of a dolphin. The covering tapers out when it reaches his ankles, wrists and collar bone. Finally, allowing the tan tint of his human DNA to be revealed.

It does not take the man long to state the reasoning for his appearance, "Good evening. For those of you who do not already know, my name is Dalton. I am the ruler of this world.

First, I want to thank all of the guests visiting or traveling through our world.

Now, please remember that the rules of the realm are simple:

Rule one: Be kind to one another. Do everything with the purest intention of your soul. So, that way we can all live in peace among each other.

Rule two: Do not forget number one in every step of your existence, even when you leave here. Remember, this is not only for yourself, but most importantly those who have to surround you."

Luke can feel an intense pressure pushing against the front of his throat.

He cannot help but let the letters slow out into the air,

"And, has this ever actually worked?"

The entire room drains of all sound as Dalton tilts his head to the right, "Explain the reason for your rude and disrespectful outburst."

Luke places both of his palms together in a praying manner allowing the front half of his body to tip forward for a few moments before returning into an upright placement, "I apologize, sir. Please, forgive me. I just cannot seem to sit by while an injustice is being committed right in front of my face."

Dalton nods his head once towards my pawn in a firm motion, "What is the injustice? Tell me, now. I must fix it at once."

Luke can feel a small smile breaking against his lips, "You are forgetting the only way to really enforce this rule is to first control the mind. However, it does not stop there. Every person you meet is three entirely different streams of water that are coming together to make a beautiful pond. This represents a person as a whole.

You must get to know their mind, body and soul while not letting any of them be masked, blinding you from being able to see the truth.

Now, imagine that you meet someone who has a clear intention for both their soul and their body, but their mind is contaminated with algae such as hatred, greed, jealousy, etc.

The algae in the one stream of the mind is then going to drain and merge with the other water. What is going to happen then?

The good deeds of the other streams will delude the filth, but it will still be there causing problems in all three sections until it is filtered properly.

Always remember to make sure that all three parts of yourself are clean, stable and aligned for the greater good of yourself and others."

Dalton quickly disappears into thin air from the stage, reappearing on the mortals' tabletop. Now, standing at a mere five-inches tall.

His voice startles my pawns, "What is your name?"

Luke's head snaps in a fast, downwards movement, "Luke."

Dalton nods once in understanding, "Okay, Luke. I request that you and your friends come stay with me in my world. I would like you to continue to comfort and bring peace to my people with your words. Please, I am begging you."

Luke shakes his head gently, "No. I apologize, but I cannot stay. I am currently on my way to save a friend. I must stay focused on my commitment. It is only fair."

I can see the disappointment draining from his chiseled, strong facial structure, "I understand. Thank you, Luke for teaching me something earlier tonight that I might not have figured out on my own."

Luke flashes him a half, right sided grin, "Yes, you would have. You are very smart. All you have to do is remain calm. The right answers will always be presented to those who take the time to try to understand a situation or person before just reacting."

Dalton slightly bows to my humans before disappearing from sight.

Luke turns his attention towards Emily, "Grab Austin, let's go."

CHAPTER SEVEN:

Luke begins leading the others towards the hotel rooms, a slight yawn is stolen from his throat, "I am really tired, all of the sudden. I think that it was the tea."

Austin nods his head slowly in agreement with the statement as Emily whispers, "Me too."

Luke seems to have a pep in his step now that he knows sleep is in his near future, "We can go explore the ship more when we wake up from our nap."

Their exhausted forms finally make it to their temporary, bedroom doors.

Austin's face drains to a sickly white as he slides both of his hands out of his front pockets.

He tosses his head back in a state of irritation, "Great! Now, I have to go find a member of the crew."

Emily's tone scrapes against his ears, "Why? What is wrong?"

Austin shakes his head, "I think I left the key to the lock in the room. I'll have to find someone who can open it."

Luke extends his open, right palm towards Austin, "No. You can sleep on the couch in our room, if you want."

Austin tilts his facial structure to the left, "Are you sure that is okay?"

Emily waves her right wrist in a playful manner, "Of course. It is no big deal. Then when we wake up, we will all go to get a new key together."

Austin flashes them both a fast smile before they all disappear into the door frame on the left side of the hall.

I am unsure how much time has passed until now.

The sound of creatures roaming the halls of the ship cause Austin's mind to begin tuning into the reality that surrounds him.

He pulls the upper-half of his body into a sitting position giving his eyes a moment to readjust.

Right now, his vision is currently placed on a dark green, velvety blanket that allows hunks of the burgundy couch beneath to show through.

He can feel the heavy lock of sleep still hanging in the corners of his vision.

He uses the tips of his right fingers to remove the gooey debris, hoping to give clarity to his vision.

His eyes fall against Luke and Emily's bed. The rhythm of his heart begins to pound at a rapid pace seeing that Luke is nowhere to be found.

He quickly uses his right hand to remove the entanglement of covers from his flushed form.

The heavy structure of his feet connecting with the short, gray carpeting causes Emily to awaken as well.

She greets him with a groggy tone, "Good morning."

Austin's mind is on a completely different topic, "Where is Luke? He is not in the room."

Emily runs her right fingers in a backwards motion through her tangled strands, "Are you sure he is not in the room?"

Austin scans the area in one, fast glance, "There is only one bed, a couch and a small bathroom by the door. He is not in here. Do you know where he might have gone?"

Emily throws her torso into a fast, upright position, "I have no idea. Maybe, he went to go explore the ship."

Austin's words leak with anxiety, "Come on, let's go check."

CHAPTER EIGHT:

Austin leads Emily back up the darkened flight of stairs.

His stride is rushed, taking two steps at a time.

He calls back over his left shoulder in a state of authority, "Maybe, he came up here to talk to the crew."

Emily can only nod her head in agreement as fear has locked her voice solely to her mind.

Warm rays of sun light graze against their forms as they break free from the tunnel-like chamber and out onto the top deck.

They find themselves moving at a fast jog, not wanting to waste a single second.

The Captain steps out of her space, nearly smacking into them by accident as they zoom past, "Slow down, guys. What is the hurry?"

Austin and Emily both dig their heels into the wooden panels underneath their weight.

Austin attempts to find his voice between gasps of air, "We can't find Luke. Please, tell me you've seen him."

She tips her head back slightly in thought, "No, I have not. When did you see him last?"

Emily trips over the movements of her tongue, "Last

night, when we went to sleep. This morning when Austin woke up, he was gone."

The Captain inhales deeply allowing the molecules of air to completely engulf her, "I was afraid that this was going to happen. When the crew told me how Dalton reacted to Luke at dinner, I wondered if they would attempt to get information out of him."

Austin's bottom lip shakes as he speaks, "What kind of information are they wanting?"

She exhales loudly, "Knowledge."

Emily's voice shatters against the currents of air, "Where is he?"

The Captain gently uses the tip of her tongue to moisten her bottom lip, "Everything exists on different levels of vibrations. If you really want to find him in the physical worlds, you must first find him in your own world."

Emily raises both of her open palms towards the sides of her head in a distressed manner, "I couldn't even tell you where I am in my own little world, it is such a mess. How am I ever going to find him?"

Before the Captain has a chance to offer a reply, Austin steps forward, "I am sorry, but Emily's feelings are valid. I feel the same way. Could you better explain to us how we can find him?"

The Captain nods her head gently, "If you would like, I can guide you through your journey."

Emily's eyes ignite into a sea of sparkles, "You would really do that?"

The Captain releases a small chuckle, "Of course. Let me go find one of my crew members to take over while I am gone. I will be right back."

CHAPTER NINE:

Once the Captain finds a temporary replacement for her shift, she begins to reappear in my vision receptors.

She smiles widely at my humans as the space between them starts to close quickly, "If you are ready to continue, I would like you both to follow me. So, we can get stated."

Once she sees their heads move forward in confirmation. She quickly turns on her heels to lead the way.

The intensity of her vibration is shot in my pawns' direction.

Austin leans into Emily whispering softly, "She is very happy. I always wished that I could be happy like that."

Emily's voice is barely decipherable as it leaves her vocal cords in a weak stream, "Me too."

Their attention is shot forward, towards the sound of a wooden door creaking open.

Their pupils reflect the image of the Captain holding open a door that leads into a space filled with unknown darkness.

She urges them to enter before her, with a gentle wave of her right wrist.

Even with her offering them nothing but compassion, they still find themselves remaining cautious, only advancing two, small strides past the threshold.

The Captain follows Emily's footprints, reaching her arm behind Emily's frame to flip on the light.

The soft glow of a yellow bulb illuminates the area, both of my pawns' mouths drop open in response.

Different size pillows are covered in many hues and patterns scattered around the floor with no rhythm to their placement.

Pushed up against the right wall is a dark stained, wooden table that is roughly eight-feet long and two-feet wide. Its height is equal to Austin's hip.

Austin feels himself being pulled in that direction. His eyes expand in awe as he admires all of the whimsical items placed on top.

Emily's mind becomes directed in the opposite path, four-feet away, towards three tapestries. They are laying side by side, expanding the entire twelve-feet of wall space from front to back. Each one is scrolled with a spiritual muse.

The mixture of calming Earth colors intertwines with the fabric, carrying her soul to a vibration of momentary inner peace.

Her concentration is shattered by the Captain, "Okay, guys. If I could please get you to take off your shoes and find a place to sit on the ground, we will begin. Thank you."

Both of my pawns begin to follow her instructions, plopping themselves down into the sea of cushions.

Emily can feel a question burning against the back of her

throat, but she fears asking, not wanting to seem uneducated.

Finally, a gust of courage pushes the words free, "Captain, what is all of this stuff in here used for?"

The Captain exhales deeply, "Please. Try not to worry yourself too much with what we will be doing in the future. Everything you need to know will be answered in time either by me or yourselves."

Austin and Emily both nod slowly in response trying to give everything the time it needs to fully allow the information they already learned to finish sinking in.

The Captain smiles gently in their direction, "The only thing I need from you right now is to just close your eyes and try to relax. You will be able to hear me walking around you and you might even start to pick up on a new aroma. Do not be alarmed. I am just going to be clearing your energy. If you find yourself having any questions or concerns during the process, please ask right away, so you do not forget."

It does not surprise me that a question is already building inside of Austin.

He slowly raises his left hand to gather her attention.

She acknowledges him by nodding once in his directive path, "Yes?"

His voice is now two times deeper than its normal pitch, "What are you going to be doing exactly?"

She allows the soft flow of her tone to bounce around their zone, "All you have to do right this moment is relax and I will explain more while I am doing the work. Trust me, I understand that this task I have given you for the time being is not easy to adjust to, if you are used to handling every situation in a state of panic and anxiety. Please, just keep trying to master it and do not give up on yourselves."

Emily and Austin both nod allowing the weight of their lids to cover the area of the surroundings.

The Captain stands. She walks in a counterclockwise manner around the duo, reaching her open palms into the space around their forms. She does not allow herself too close to them physically, keeping her flesh three-inches from their figures.

She appears to be grabbing at something invisible to my uneducated visual receptors.

Once she is sure she has a firm grasp around the invisible matter, she throws it behind her back to have it be released into the air.

A deep inhale of salty air invades her lungs, "I am currently cleaning the energy field around you. It—"

Austin feels a question shooting up from his throat, "We have energy fields around us?"

The weight of her head bobs forward, "You might be able to understand clearer if I call it an aura. Everything around us and we, ourselves are nothing but energy. We know that. Science on Earth has known that for many years. However, they have yet to understand fully why and how we are able to be here on a physical plane and what the purpose of all of this is. The Divine is energy, you were created in this image. You are essentially a walking lure, catching everything you think, feel and do onto your line.

Whether you want to accept this or not, a lot of things that happened to you that you would consider negative is your own responsibility. This is not to be confused with the situation itself happening, but rather the way and how long you allowed it to control you and your inner peace."

Austin nods his head slowly, "So, the Divine is just energy?"

A fast response falls from her bottom lip, "Yes."

I can see the anxiety moving along his eyes beneath the fleshy cover of his lids as he scans his brain for another question he can feel beginning to build, "What else do you know about the Divine?"

CHAPTER TEN:

The Captain releases a small chuckle, "That is a very good question. A lot of people want to know more about our creator, it is perfectly normal. I will tell you want I have learned from my experience. We are a soul that could be thousands of years old. You are not mortal. You are not a human. You are a soul living as a human, to be able to learn faster on the physical plane.

Before coming down here, you went to the Divine and asked for a body. You got to pick your life and decide which lessons you wanted to learn in order to do your soul work. You also had the option of when and how far apart the lessons would be given to you.

We were never actually born and we will never die, we only transition. Energy cannot be destroyed, only contained. We come here to fight and overcome emotional, mental and physical struggles within ourselves, not other people.

We all come down here with spirit guide(s) and angel(s), who help us remember who we truly are and what we are supposed to be doing here for our greatest good as well as for others."

The Captain refrains from speaking momentarily, drinking up a small breath of air, "Do you have any other questions?"

I can sense that they are still trying to process all of this new information. They only both shake their heads in response.

A small smirk begins to carve itself into the right side of her mouth, "Okay, then. We will continue on. When you think of your relationship with the Divine, you should not be afraid of it. If you are feeling afraid, you are unable to expand your current mindset and it could hold you back from unlocking your true connective abilities. The Divine loves you very much and wants you to be safe, happy and healthy. This relationship is to build your connection to the source as well as to aid you in your inner growth.

Everything is going according to plan and will move with ease once you realign with the Divine and other souls. Before you came down here, you were given goals and lessons to accomplish. Part of this plan is to fully become aware of everything.

The only thing you can take with you through time and space is your soul. The work you do spiritually in this life will follow you into your future. It is very important that we go through this process when we are as young as possible. You do not want to have to wait until you are old to be wise. Save yourself years of trouble and be wise today."

Emily's eyes begin to flicker open.

She sees the Captain is now sitting in front of them, "What do we have to do to be able to reach this Divine connection? I would like this information. The truth, to be able to better serve the soul in all of us."

Austin's fluttering vision captures my interest, "I want to be able to find answers to better myself and others with all emotional and mental struggles. I want to find peace."

The Captain nods her head once in a calming motion, "I will teach you everything you need to know to be able to reach your higher self. All of the goals, dreams and love you crave, will be presented for your hard work. Please, before we go any further down this journey together, I would like to disclose some information.

This path is going to change everything about you. It is going to alter the way you look at yourself and the way you view others. It is going to dissect every thought, emotion and action you have and replace them with a higher energy vibration. Every person in your life will start to shift with you, some will rise as well and others will fall away because they are not yet ready to take on this change. Yourself love, confidence, inner strength and motivation will be set to overdrive while all negativity will just start to fade away.

Life is not hard. In fact, for a calm brain, life is easy. All of the changes are for a positive shift, but sometimes transitioning can be a little tricky. I need you guys to follow my instructions. At least, give them a fair shot when advice is given to lessen the pain of a situation. Even when it sounds scary or hard to accomplish.

Once you start down this path, you will not be able to go back. Every step you take in the right direction, your soul grows. Once the shift starts, you will feel different. When situations start to arise inside of you, I will be there to help you through. You have no need to worry, all of these changes will improve your life.

I just need both of you to give me a firm confirmation that you do in fact want these alterations to occur."

Austin does not allow another moment of time to be wasted, "Yes, I do."

Emily quickly nods in agreement, "I do as well."

The Captain's smile breaks as words escape through her parted lips, "Great, then we will start right away. That is, if you are sure."

CHAPTER ELEVEN:

The Captain leans her weight forward, adjusting the placement of her crossed legs, "The Divine is everywhere around us, held encased along every single one of the creations. Every single piece serves a purpose, they all also hold a part of wisdom that we can learn from. Some creations hold more than others, but all bear great power.

Imagine that you are back on Earth and the only thing in front of you is a tree. I want you to walk around this tree, admiring it from different angles, looking at it without judgement or limitations. Once you start to do this, you will see Divine magic everywhere you look. Now, in your own opinion, what do you currently think of when you see a tree?"

Austin is the first to offer up a response, "Oxygen."

Emily nods her head in agreement to his thought, "Life."

The Captain nods slowly, "Great. Those are both very true. Now, I am going to share with you some lessons I have been taught by the trees. While they are being transferred to you, listen only to the information to fully download it into your mind to be processed for later, so no interruptions cause the knowledge to become distorted.

This is something that in order to master it fully, you will need some practice. If you do not get it on the first try, be gentle with yourself. It is okay to make a mistake, just do not allow it to prevent your growth.

Now, when I first started my own journey and was asked the question about the tree, my response was similar to yours. Today, if someone were to ask me that same question, I would say that I see a home for many different creatures as well as myself. I see the branches as a reflection of our brain having the ability to branch out as far as it wishes as long as we remain grounded to the current reality we are in. It teaches us the cycle of birth, life and death. It allows us to accept that we, too will transition a lot throughout life. Sometimes, multiple shifts will occur in a one-year phase. It teaches us to let go of things that no longer are fulfilling what we have to do in order to properly serve ourselves and others. A tree would not bear life if it was always worried about the leaves it had already lost. It teaches that what covers our form does not define us or our beauty. It blooms food, in order for us to survive. Only asking for love and care in return for its generosity. The tree does not judge who it is able to serve, whether it be a creature, a man of color, a woman in power, an elderly man or a small child. It does not matter what tongue you speak, we all feel hunger. In times of our greatest need, the trees are there to offer us a way to reconnect and recharge the Divine energy within all of us."

A small pause begins to form in the air, it surrounds them as a gentle laugh is released from her lungs, "I know that all of this is a lot of information. I do not want to overload your minds with too much at one time. I am going to take a small break and go get us some tea to drink. It will help relax your body and mind during the first steps of transformation. When I am gone, if the two of you want to start processing the information we already discussed. I will answer any questions you may have when I return."

CHAPTER TWELVE:

The Captain hands both of my pawns a cream colored, ceramic coffee mug.

A light caramel hue engulfs the molecules as they swim along fresh lavender petals.

Austin allows a few drops of the intoxicating aroma to trail against his taste buds, "So, are you saying that all of the bad things that happened to me are my fault?"

A deep breath is pushed from the Captain's lungs, "Well, it depends. We would have to go through every specific scenario that you have ever experienced, talk about it and then I would be able to make a fair judgement based off the information to help you figure out if it is karma or simply a sleeping mind."

Emily allows her vision to squish together slightly, "What is the difference between a sleepy mind and karma?"

A soft pause forms momentarily in the air, Emily quickly fills it with another question, "Also, could you please explain what a *sleeping mind* means?"

The Captain smiles in a gentle manner, "You will be able to tell the difference because in a karmatic situation there is no right answer. For example, let's say you are walking down the street and a man comes up behind you, putting a gun to your head. Then he tells you that you either get shot in the head with the gun or you have to inject a drug into your system and if you do, you will be free.

Immediately, you would be able to tell that this is karma because either option has a negative effect. If and when you find yourself in this type of situation, always go with the one that causes the least pain to you and others. In this case, you would rather take the drug and be set free.

Now, a sleeping mind is when a human body is being ran by the mind instead of the soul. We will discuss that more in depth at a later time.

Those were great questions so far, is there anymore? I want to make sure you understand everything fully about a topic before we move on. This is more than just knowing the information, it is exploring the knowledge and becoming one with it."

Austin slowly nods his head forward, hoping to capture her attention, "Could you explain to me how much freewill we actually have in the physical plane? I know this must sound like a very odd question, but I have always wondered if the Divine is in complete control or not. I guess, I just want to make sure I am doing the best I can for myself and others."

The Captain flashes him a loving graze, "Austin, no question is weird. Never feel strange for asking about something. You were born to grow and expand in every way possible. Okay, so for the question.

Yes, the Divine and the universe are very much in control. They are in charge of ensuring that we have dealt with our karma, our soul contracts, etc. They set everything up for us along the path. Your freewill is how gracefully you follow this trail. You control the journey, just like in this world we are currently in. Our thoughts effect the trip. Either way, we will make it from point A to B, that is the Divine. However, whether the ride is smooth or chaos, that is up to us."

Both of my pawns feel themselves becoming calm and intrigued by this information.

They can only nod their heads in response to their brain's overload of thoughts.

The Captain allows her voice the ability to once again flow freely around the room, "Do either of you have any more questions or concerns?"

They respond in a rhythmic vocal expression between each other, "No."

A small laugh creeps up the back of the Captain's throat, "Okay, then. With that being the end of this half of the lesson, we are going to move onto something really great. I think you guys will enjoy it."

CHAPTER THIRTEEN:

I allow my attention to drift towards Austin and Emily.

They are in a whirl of amazement, listening to the Captain talk, "The next thing I want you to open is your mind, heart and soul to your spiritual guides and angels. We are not sent here alone. We have help. You know that soft whisper of a voice you hear in your mind that sounds like it is yours, yet it is different? That is your guide. Everyone has at least one, some people have up to thirty. It all just depends on the job you came here to do.

When we are not connected to our guides, we tend to have more depression, anxiety, feeling lost, homesick, negative choices with yourself and others, poor work ethic, addictions, financial trouble, etc.

An easier way for you to look at them is by understanding what they are doing.

I want both of you to imagine your best friend in your mind, allow all of the love in your soul for this person to flood through every inch of your existence. Do you have it?"

They both nod gently in response.

The Captain straightens her posture, "Great. Now, imagine that this person woke up tomorrow and could not remember a thing about themselves, their life or other people. Everything they knew is completely gone.

You would want to be there for them, all the time. Teach them everything you know about situations and themselves. You would want them to be safe, happy and healthy. You would give them advice when they need a gentle nudge forward. You would steer them only towards positive energies. When they cry, you would hold them and whisper kind words to sooth their discomfort. If they could not get out of bed one morning, you would be the one to convince them why they are worth living another day with eyes wide open. You would be there to remind them of the value that they bring to the world just by existing. You would be protective of the people in their life as you would not want anything to take advantage of their situation.

The way you would look at and treat your best friend through that situation, is how your guide is going to respond to you. They will never misguide you.

Now, I know you cannot really understand talking with your guide, right now. I will help you reach that point later in the story, but right now I want you to get used to seeing them and interacting with their energy. So, I am going to introduce you to mine."

My mind is suddenly being pulled towards Emily and Austin's energy which is stronger than usual due to the excitement being emitted from their forms.

The Captain also notices their shift in energy which in return sparks a flame inside of her, "Yes. I thought that you guys would enjoy this part of the lesson. I am happy to see this kind of reaction. Austin, will you put one of your hands underneath mine. Emily, will you do the same motion, but on the top."

The shuffling of fabric from the pillows shifting under their weight scrapes against my hearing. My vision remains strong against the Captain, who already has her right hand extended away from her form.

The moment their flesh touches hers, a gasp is stolen from their throats.

Their eyes move in a fast, side to side movement as they scan a new member of the room in a vertical motion.

Inside of the reflective surface of their pupils, I am able to see a three-foot-tall monk. Parts of his tan skin can be seen from underneath his robe which matches his bright green eyes perfectly.

The Captain can feel their energy coursing through the room.

She attempts to re-center them, "Austin, Emily. I would like you to meet one of my guides. This is Duj."

They throw their heads in the direction of one another in awe before turning their attention back onto the flashes of stars they can see in his eyes.

Austin is finding that it is difficult to release words from his mouth, "What does he all assist you with?"

The Captain beams with love for her guide, "Anything that he feels I need help with at the time. Some are warnings about places and people. Some is guidance for luck or money. Honestly, the possibilities are limitless and unique to each individual. Trust that you will be given all of the right information at the perfect time."

Emily can feel her vocal expression shake as she attempts to reply, "That is amazing. How long will you get to keep him around you?"

The Captain allows her head to tip to the right, "For the rest of this journey. Sometimes, guides can come and go during specific times in your life to assist you, but you will never be alone. Always remember that you are safe, you are loved and you are powerful."

I can tell that they are both held in complete captivation by the situation.

The Captain smiles kindly towards them with understanding wrapped around every letter, "We will be able to discuss all of this and more at a later time. We still have many topics yet to go over. Before we change directions, do either of you have any questions?"

Emily scoots her weight forward slightly, "How do we get in touch with our guides?"

The Captain's smile flickers gently against her lips, "Before you make up your mind about whether or not you will want to walk down this path, I have one more area to cover with you, first."

CHAPTER FOURTEEN:

I watch the Captain retract her form away from my pawns, breaking their small bridge to a higher vibration.

She inhales a deep breath of neutralized air, "The energy field that I was trying to cleanse on you during your entrance into this journey is formed by energy ports around your form. We have many, but the ones I want to briefly discuss with you right now is the main seven. They are located on the outside of your physical body, ranging from the top of your head to below the groin.

They are how we process things. It controls our mental state, our emotions, our self-control and most importantly our love.

Everything you do passes through these energy filters. When they become unbalanced, we can feel it in every area of our lives and others can pick up on these shifts as well.

During the process of cleansing and maturing your energy, there are a lot of things that are going to change and shift. Your relationship to the Divine will be stronger and any spiritual gifts you have will start to come into focus. This journey is like walking into a whole different world.

Before you make a decision, think about it extremely well. Once you start, you cannot go back."

Austin instantly turns his head towards Emily, "What do you think? Should we do it?"

Emily's focus remains on the Captain, in search of her own answers, "What are the risks associated with going down this path?"

The Captain tips her head forward, "There is no risk. Everything about this journey is positive. The only way you will regret it, is if you do not give it a try. What is the worst thing that could happen? You either try it and if it does not work out for you then you stay the same as you are right now. However, if you try it and it works, things will only get better from here."

Emily takes a deep breath, "Is it scary?"

The Captain drops her vision slightly giving herself a moment to try to process the proper answer, "Scary? No. It is not something to fear. The journey itself is teaching you how to end all fear. When we finally release the fear, it is the moment we understand freedom. If anything, this path can be described as uplifting, transforming, inspiriting, healing, loving and blissful.

The constant state of fear that you are currently living in is completely unnecessary, even in your current condition.

There is no reason to fear anything. You are the greatest pieces of the Divine. When you tap into and open the connection, it is powerful enough to alter the entire world that is and will be.

Now, I would like to ask you again. Are you ready to fully commit to this change in every area of your life?

Please, take all of the time you need to think it over."

Emily blinks multiple times in a fast manner, pulling her attention out of her thoughts and onto Austin, "What are you thinking about all of this? It sounds like a great way to save ourselves and Arlenm."

Austin exhales sharply, "How are you so sure this is going to work? Will it truly make me feel better, even after all I've been through?"

Emily pans her vision towards the Captain, nodding her

head in agreement with his thought process, "We both have been through such different experiences. Will both of us get the same results in the end?"

The Captain's smile does not waiver in front of their doubt, "Yes. It tailors itself to the journey of the individual. Your path itself will be unique, but the end will always be the same."

Emily attempts to release some of her fear by a breath of air, "Austin, I want to do this."

He uses his right hand to stroke his beard as he thinks over the options, "You are right. I don't see what it would hurt. Plus, think about all of the worlds we have already survived. Whatever this one holds, we will get through that, too."

They nod once in a silent motion of understanding with each other before tiling their attention onto the Captain.

They speak in a breathless harmony, "We are ready to help ourselves and many others."

CHAPTER FIFTEEN:

The Captain is now positioned by the table that Austin was so interested in when they first arrived. She is grabbing multiple items off of the top. She is careful on her advancement back towards her seating placement.

Once she gets into a comfortable structure, she extends her right hand out towards my mortals.

The lines of her palm are facing towards the ceiling as she is now holding two, red stones.

She speaks in a relaxed tone, "This is a jasper stone. Please, pick one. It does not matter which they are the same. Now, I want you to place it underneath yourself. Make sure it is aligned with the center of your body.

Stones and crystals are very powerful and they have the ability to help make the energy in the portals continue to flow smoothly.

I want you to place yourselves into a state of meditation while still mindfully listening to some information about this energy point.

If it is out of balance, you might feel as though your emotions and thoughts are uncontrollable. You might want to run away but have no idea where you want to go, you just have the feeling of wanting to escape.

When we are balancing this point, different thoughts and emotions will come to the surface. Some of them you might have had to deal with before and some will be new.

During this current time, since you cannot speak with your guides right now. I would like you to share your situations with me, so I can advise you until your connection with your higher self has matured.

Right now, I want you to just relax and when something comes to mind, raise your right hand or give me some form of a signal and I will tap into your energy to help you along the way.

Does all of this make sense so far? Do you have any questions?"

Austin shakes his head in excitement, "I am good."

The Captain turns her attention onto Emily, who nods in agreement.

The Captain smiles briefly, "Great. Then let's begin. It is important to know that we are all connected as one. The things you heal in yourself today, could simultaneously heal another tomorrow."

CHAPTER SIXTEEN:

My attention has been on the minds of my mortals as I patiently wait for something significant to reveal itself.

Austin is the first one to begin showing any signs of mental or emotion discomfort.

His face tightens sharply, pushing his cheekbones in an upwards movement.

The Captain and I immediately find ourselves tapping into his energy.

The fast breath of Austin's voice blows through his mind, 'You are going to end up completely alone. No one cares about you. You are worthless. No one would even notice if you were dead or alive.'

He can instantly feel the effects of the negative thoughts and what they are doing to him mentally, spiritually and physically.

Before he has a chance to process what is going on with himself on the inside. He feels the boat sway roughly to the right, throwing his body into a forward shove of discomfort.

The Captain telepathically translates a phrase of positive words, 'Austin, try to stay calm. I am going to talk you through this. Take a deep breath. Before we begin, I want you to try and regain your composure. The more stable your energy is, the stronger you will be when you start fighting back against those voices.'

Austin can feel the download of information beginning to sprout new questions, 'What am I fighting exactly? Is it some form of a dark entity?'

The Captain does not waste any time organizing her thoughts, 'No, Austin. It is much more than that. Right now, you are going to start fighting yourself. The voice you just heard is negativity that you have gathered from either other people or parts of your life where your ego became damaged which forced you to put up higher walls. Instead of taking the time to fix yourself. By these things happening, you only become more engulfed by the darkness inside of you. During this time, you are going to be introduced to the worst parts of your human side. Be ready, Austin. It is going to be one hell of a ride."

All of the sudden, everything goes black. The dim light from the room that gently illuminated his lids to a soft orange is now gone, pulling him further into the depths of his mind.

A purple sphere of light hovers in the center of his mind. Its strong energy begins to coax him inside of the swirling, energy point inside of the circle.

He finds himself standing in a vision that is playing out against the screen constructed from his lids.

The clip portrays himself sitting all alone in a house that is located in some suburban neighborhood, staring out at the flakes of falling snow.

He looks down at his entangled fingers, tears start to trail down the back of his hands as he speaks out loud to himself, "I am sixty-two years old and not a single person would know if I woke up tomorrow."

Austin feels the vessel jerking sharply from side to side trying to avoid the thrashing waves crashing into the front of the boat. The force causes his body to slam into the wall behind him, cracking his head against the wooden panel.

The sound of the Captain's voice trails through the screen, shattering it into a million pieces that transform into rain droplets upon impact, falling out of the corner of his eyes, 'That is not true, Austin. You know that is not the truth. Every time thoughts like that start coming up, I want you to immediately tell your mind in a firm manner, 'No. I am loved. I am safe. I am full of the Divine light. I am complete. I am worthy of all beautiful things, including love from others.'

Austin shakes his head slowly, *'I don't want to just control it. I want to destroy it. How do I achieve this?'*

It does not take long for the Captain to chime back in, 'It is possible. However, to get to that state, you need to first destroy all fear that resides inside of yourself.'

Austin can feel a branch of this emotion creeping up the back of his throat, 'How do I destroy this fear?'

The Captain gives him the right to pick the outcome of the answer, 'Would you like information on how to solve all fear or just this one?'

Austin hears his subconscious release a nervous laugh, 'Is both an option?'

The Captain cannot hold down a growing smile, *'Yes. Okay, when you feel yourself becoming afraid, you will start to have a negative reaction in some form or another. Maybe, your vibration drops or your mind will start pouring with negative thoughts. Maybe, you become restless, sometimes even angry. Those are just a few of the signs that you will learn. Soon, you will begin to recognize more on your own as you go along the rest of the journey.*

When you start to feel the side effects of fear, immediately stop what you are doing and carefully evaluate why you are feeling that way. Once you know what you are facing, you can educate yourself on the topic. In return, you will feel more in control of the situation because now that you are educated about it, you will automatically become more relaxed.

For example:

From what you were experiencing moments ago, it is clear that it was brought on by fear.

Now, after looking over the situation, it is also clear that you are afraid of being alone.

You can build confidence within yourself on this topic by reminding yourself that you are never alone. Your guides are with you every second. They love you unconditionally. You are safe. You need to learn how to sit with yourself and just be content being, Austin. Once you master solitude, you will never have a worry about who walks in or out of your life ever again because you will know that your inner peace is in you as well as the Divine's love.

This knowledge now gives you a safety net to fall back on when another situation that is similar arises.

It will. They have to make sure that you fully learned this lesson before you can move onto the next.

The more you listen to your own voice and your guides, life becomes easy.

Everyone deserves a healthy body, a calm mind and a soul that only radiates love. Yes, Austin. Even you deserve this.'

A trail of tears run against Austin's cheeks. He quickly raises his right, index finger to wipe away the droplets.

He places his hands back into a meditative placement with his right laying inside of his left which is currently collecting his release of discomfort, *'Thank you, Captain. You have brought clarity to me as for knowing how to break myself free from this area of my past.'*

The Captain tries to conceal a small smile, *'You are welcome. You are doing great. Remember, if something does come up, do not be afraid. Trust that all you have to do is find a way to make it irrational.'*

It has been an hour since Austin has shown any signs of suffering.

The Captain and I can sense a rapid shift in his energy. We immediately jump into the currents that surround him, making sure that we do not miss a single second of his growth.

Austin's brain activity is shooting across his neurons at a fast pace, 'I wonder if we are ever going to find Arlenm? I hope Luke is okay. I wonder if we are ever going to get out of the game. What if we make it to the end, but Arlenm still does not let us leave?'

His thoughts start to crumble as his attention is shot towards the rapid pound of his heartbeat. His air supply becomes shallow and slow. The energy coursing along his physical form is far too intense for him to ignore. His limbs ache in restlessness as a side effect of his current frequency. His feelings only begin to multiply as the ship begins rocking back and forth causing the boards of the creation to moan and creak.

The Captain tries to offer words of comfort, 'Sometimes, when we find ourselves attempting to resist the natural flow of the universe, strange things can start to occur in our life.

If you feel yourself in a state of paranoia, fear, feeling empty or over all out of sorts. It is because you are living in the future tense of fear which in return will give you horrible anxiety.'

Austin releases a small chuckle, *'Yes. I do have a lot of anxiety. Do you have any advice on how I can cure it? I will try anything. I am that desperate.'*

The Captain raises the vibration of her tone, offering him comfort, 'I do understand how difficult it can be to live in a state of constant, repetitive fear. When it comes to things happening outside of your control, whether that be meeting people, careers, lessons, relationships, etc. I am not saying to not try, but stressing about the outcome of these sort of things is not going to help anything. It is only going to make the journey difficult when it does not have to be.

Focus only on the outcome you desire. Forget any other options even exist. Put all of your attention into the Divine, into the universe, into karma and go about your path in peace. Otherwise, it will leave you in pieces.'

Austin tips his head forward, *'Thank you.'*

The Captain's smile flicks in and out, *'I am not saying this is going to be easy. Adapting to this new mindset and all, but I do promise that if you are truly in search of change, it works.'*

Austin's head falls to the left slightly, *'How long do you think it will take for it to go away for good?'*

A deep breath is pushed from the chamber of the Captain's lungs, *'That all depends on you. How firm you are when you confront it and how badly you never want to feel that way again.'*

It does not take him long to quiet down. Once we are sure no questions are going to arise anytime soon. We remove ourselves from his energy field, waiting for the next spark of pain.

The next round of bullets seems to be coming at him quicker than the last.

With us now being intertwined with his brain structure, we instantly feel the effects of his shift.

Austin whines under the pressure of anger rocketing through his head.

His fists ball into a white knuckled grip, *'I can feel the anger running through my form. I want to stop it, but I do not know how. All I want to do is punch a hole through the wall.'*

The veins protrude from his forearms as he tries to steady his form, feeling the boat rocking violently from side to side as a harsh wind blows against the sails above.

The Captain raises her hands gently, *'Austin, please calm down. There is no reason that you should be holding onto this emotion so tightly. What is it that caused you to feel this way?'*

Austin inhales deeply, hoping the air will cleanse his thoughts, *'To be honest, there are times that I don't have an answer until I evaluate it after the damage is already done. It makes me feel horrible, I don't mean for this type of release to be happening. Is there any advice you could give me?'*

The Captain smiles, leaning forward slightly, *'Next time you feel anger trying to harm you or someone else, immediately shift your thoughts, removing yourself from the situation. Take a few moments to decide how you want to react.*

We have the right at any moment to ask for a break to think about something. If you made a decision and you want to change your mind because the situation you agreed to before compromises your mind, body or soul you can do that as well. You are the one who is in control of your thoughts, emotions and actions. When you feel a negative emotion, never blame something else for bringing it up. Blame yourself for not stopping it.'

Austin exhales sharply as the shot of truth is a little much for him to bear, *'Thank you for looking at the possibilities of change within me.'*

A fast reply leaves the Captain's soul, 'I would not have been able to see it in you, if you had not seen it first.'

With the room now covered in a blanket of silence. I can tell that the Captain is beginning to feel the side effects that the negative pull has on her entire state.

I lean my weight against my right leg, "Is everything okay?"

The Captain turns her head towards me as the smile runs from my lips.

A single thought trails against my brain, 'She can see me?'

Another thought enters just as fast, except this one is from the

Captain, 'And, hear you, too.'

I exhale deeply, shaking my head slightly trying to break the energy alignment she has on me.

A fast smile runs against the right side of her mouth, "I am fine, thank you. The episodes or flashes of emotion he is experiencing will eventually start to fade."

I tilt my attention towards Emily, still directing my voice for the Captain, "Why isn't she being tortured like Austin is?"

The Captain straightens her shoulders slightly, "She will. He just had a little bit more happen to him, so he is experiencing the cleansing at a more rapid level. Do not worry, she will catch up."

Before I have a chance to ask any more questions, our attention is shot towards Austin's stomach growling for his aid.

We immediately mend our minds with his, hoping that we will be able to assist.

I can feel his body react to our presence in his space. He responds to our frequencies by melting into a relaxed state.

The Captain nods her head once in a silent greeting towards Austin, *'What is it that you are hearing?'*

Austin shakes his head gently, *'I don't know if I want to tell you. This is different than the rest so far.'*

The Captain beams with love and compassion for his situation, 'I have been through a lot in my existence as well. I understand that some things are difficult to share, but in order for your pain to be transformed into something that helps you and others, it needs to be open. That thing that hurt you will no longer be pain, but growth.'

Austin releases a deep breath, *'I keep hearing that I am overweight.'*

A small silence creeps across the space before he tries to add more depth to the explanation, 'I know that I am not. I also know that fear is irrational, yet I have not been able to eat in peace for years.'

The Captain nods in a slow motion of understanding, *'I get what you mean. I went through something similar, myself. Tell yourself every day that you are a healthy weight. That you are handsome. That your weight does not define you, with or without it. This sounds like a very simply method. However, it will only work if you truly believe in your own inner power.'*

Austin releases a doubtful laugh, 'You know. This all sounds so easy. I am having a difficult time believing that any of this is even true.'

The Captain tips her head to the right, *'Was it easy while you were going through it?'*

Austin shakes his head in a firm response, *'No. It was really challenging. At times, I did not think I was going to make it.'*

The Captain smiles gently in his direction, *'Once you figured it out, it became easy, just like everything in life. Practice is the key to getting a new mindset to stick as well.'*

Austin's mind is starting to feel less cloudy, 'Why doesn't everyone do these things? It would make life so much brighter for so many people.'

The Captain nods in understanding of his concern, *'They can only discover the answers when they seek them. A lot of people consider their feelings to be, 'normal' while that is to an extent true, they are not seeing a problem in their behavior. We have to remain calm and confident that when their time to break through that barrier comes, they will. Until then, we just do the best we can every single day.'*

CHAPTER SEVENTEEN:

Now that Austin's energy has calmed, the Captain feels a pull, dragging her towards Emily.

We both connect our brain currents with hers, hoping to gain insight to what is going on.

Emily's mind floods with a downpour of negative thoughts, 'I wonder how Austin is doing? I bet he is really far ahead of me. I wonder if anything is happening with him yet? Maybe, I am doing something wrong. I am feeling very insecure with myself right now. I don't know what to do.'

The frantic pound of her voice against the drums of her mind are abruptly shattered as her back slams into the wall behind her, forcing all of her attention to be geared to the air being ripped from her lungs.

The Captain allows her words to travel towards Emily, 'Please, do not listen to the things that are being said to you in a negative manner. They are there to make you fight for your inner strength. When you hear that, know your soul needs to feel love for itself. You will never fully understand why or how someone else can love you until you love yourself. If you find yourself believing those things all it means is that you need more self-love.'

Emily can feel the weight of her shoulders pull into a backwards response, *'I know that I don't have it, but I also wouldn't like myself at all, if I did have it. So, I think with this, I'll just stay how I am.'*

The Captain does not allow her smile to fade, *'What do you mean? Why would you be worse?'*

Emily can feel her confidence in the answer slipping fast from her grasp, 'I don't know. Anyone I have ever meet who claimed to 'love' themselves were not nice to themselves or others. I don't want that. I don't want to be mean.'

The Captain leans closer to her in hopes of transferring a calming energy, *'The type of self-love you are referring to is fueled by the ego. The type that I am talking about is fueled by the soul. One is to serve yourself, the other is to help yourself advance in such a way that it serves others as well. It will teach you an unconditional love for all things.'*

Emily maneuvers her weight in between the structure of her hips, *'Can you please teach me how to attain this form of balance in myself with love?'*

The Captain's head pushes forward in a motion of agreement, *'I want you to think of Luke. Do you feel how much you love him and Austin? What if you loved yourself just as much?'*

Her smile ignites under the mere thought, *'That would be amazing.'*

The Captain clears her throat slightly, *'Great. In order to achieve this, I want you from this moment on to make every single decision for yourself as if you were making it for Luke. You will start to find that as time passes, you will think of yourself and still make the same choices you would have for him. This exercise works so well because if you love yourself the way you love others, you will set yourself free from their opinions just as they would then be released from yours.'*

Emily nods gently in understanding, *'I have a question.'*

The Captain thinks over a response, 'You are safe with me and yourself. You do not have to ask. Please, speak freely during this time. Hold nothing back.'

Emily can feel a nervous energy tracking along her inner form, 'For a reason that I cannot understand, I am suddenly feeling myself becoming attached to the aspect of money. I have never had this sensation before. This random change in direction concerns me. Why is this happening and what can I do to turn it around?'

The Captain takes a moment to evaluate the advice she wishes to translate, 'When we start walking down this path, we must constantly be in a state of learning and growth. These things that are being brought to your attention want you to understand them. You have to break these scenarios apart whether they are big or small. Every drop of existence serves a purpose. The more you conquer in yourself, the brighter your light will burn in the darkness for others to help them redirect their vibrations to match yours.

Look inside of yourself until you find an answer of peace. Once something is no longer trucking along your mind, is the minute you defeated it inside of yourself.

To help aid you in this issue, I suggest reminding yourself that physical things are not permanent nor are allowed to be taken with you when you transition from this life to the next. The only thing you can take with you is your soul. That is what you should be focusing on, constantly bettering your Divine characteristics, constantly spreading love.'

CHAPTER EIGHTEEN:

My mind starts to drift back towards the Captain.

She speaks in a loud strum that irritates their ear drums, "If I could have you guys hand me back the stones that I gave you earlier, I would like to replace them with the next one that we will be working with."

Without either one pulling themselves completely out of their meditative states, they both retrieve the stone from underneath them with their dominate hand.

Once the stones are collected, the Captain lays another product of the Earth against the warm lining of their flesh, "This is a moon stone. You do not have to evaluate it with your sight. Simply allow the energy to flow through every inch of your forms. It will naturally stimulate the targeted energy port to help balance and open this current.

Again, it is unknown at this time what either of you are going to have to face within yourself once the energy starts to regulate. You are stronger than you want to believe, I will be right here if you need me."

Both of my pawns retract their hands, laying them back into their laps, keeping a loose grip on the moonstone.

The Captain and I are patiently waiting for the next round of growth to begin sprouting through the soil.

It does not take long for us to realize that Austin is starting to feel an intense energy decrease.

His form starts to shiver in reaction to something

unknown to us at the moment, playing through his thoughts.

The Captain pushes her energy forward, linking brain activity with Austin.

Thoughts are being fired in every direction, 'Maybe, everyone is right, you are worth nothing. I don't understand why you continue to wake up every morning. Nobody would notice if you were gone. No wonder Raven didn't love you. You are so weak, it is pathetic.'

A shiver runs along Austin's spine, triggering the reaction of tears to flood from the corners of his vision. Drops of the liquid pain are shot in different directions as the waves throw his figure in a swaying movement.

The Captain does not wish to see him in such a state of despair any longer, 'Austin, listen to me. Please, relax.'

He shakes his head firmly, *'I am afraid of myself. It is a horrible feeling. It is the main reason I cannot stand to be alone. My thoughts are constantly torturing me, stabbing at my wounds. I have been so low for so long, I forgot what it feels like to be high.'*

She offers him a calming tone, 'You need to try and hear what I am trying to explain. You are fighting your past. You are out of that environment. It can no longer cause you harm unless you allow it to. You are not handling the transition of life easily. It is nothing to be concerned with. I will teach you how to overcome this resistance that you are creating. A lot of people are never taught how to handle a transition, yet we all go through so many in life.

Here are some examples:
A child becoming an adult.
Moving.
School to work.
Being single to being in a relationship.

Being a couple to be a family.
Getting pets.
Losing or gaining friends.
Changing careers.
Etc.

When you find yourself feeling in a low vibration with no direct cause it is a good sign that you need to make sure you are still not trying to live in the past and the present at the same time. You have to allow yourself the green light to completely remove yourself from what you went through physically, emotionally and mentally.

This can be done by going through all of the people or events that caused you trauma and find the sections of the situation where you noticed growth within yourself.

Right now, you might not be able to see any signs of your growth, but trust me it is there. Otherwise, you would not be here. When you change your thought of depression to appreciation you will no longer be held in the chains of 'what if'. You will be able to step forward, with no baggage.

When you are no longer being controlled by your past events, it can be helpful to introduce yourself fully to the present.

Look around your reality, acknowledge how far you have come, notice the things you have already overcome within yourself. Reconnect with your family and friends. Remind yourself that right here, right now, in this moment you are safe.

It is going to take some work in the beginning, but it will not take long for you to allow the positive energy to consume you just as quickly and intensely as you did with the bad.

We are by nature very adaptable to change. Everything around us is constantly progressing. Do not resists the alterations when they start to shape into something so beautiful, it scares you.

You have two options when it comes time to transition.

Option one: either way life is going to change. If you resist this change in anyway, you will experience stress, tension, fatigue, anxiety, fear, weight loss, weight gain, restlessness, self-harm, harm to others, digestive problems, heart disease, etc. You will end up being 'dragged' through the change. You will reject it, find everything you can wrong with it, try to destroy it and even act irrationally in hopes that somehow this behavior will alter the outcome, but it will not. All you are doing is preventing your own growth, your own happiness, your own blessings.

Option two: When change starts to show signs that it is taking over, make peace with the situation as quickly as possible. This will keep you balanced and grounded through the changes. If you do this, your mind will already start accepting the alterations which will make walking into this new environment more open allowing the healing, growth, love, happiness, etc. to engulf every single inch of your life.

Do not allow your mind to keep recycling the same thoughts that will eventually manifest the exact things you are trying to escape. You learned your lesson, cherish them and then let it go. Do you think you can give this process a chance?'

Austin exhales forcibly through the slice in his parted lips, *'It is not going to be easy, even though these people and events caused me harm, I still love them. Is there any advice you have for that?'*

A moment of silence fills the space around us.

I can feel a spark of joy overtaking my form, it makes me feel as though he has finally asked a question that she cannot find an answer to, 'Great! Now, that he will see that she is unable to provide him with the complete inner peace he so deeply desires, he will return to being loyal to me and the game.'

The sound of my thoughts being processed in my ears cause a jolt of fear to run across my lips, 'Shit! She can hear my thoughts as well!'

The vibration of a soulful laugh leaves the Captain's throat in response to my actions, turning her attention onto Austin, 'Yes, Austin. I do have some information that might make letting go easier. Do you remember in the beginning when we were talking about soul contracts?'

Austin cannot contain his response, 'Yes.'

Her thoughts flow gently towards him, 'Good. When we were making our soul contract, we knew that we had some lessons we had to learn here in the physical dimension in order to be the best version of ourselves.

These people that agreed to come here and teach us the more painful of lessons, truly do love us a lot. They came here to help you outgrow them and be the greatest you can be. It is okay you love them, wish them the best, but please understand that this is a classroom. They are not meant to be in your life forever, they are a lesson. A course in which you need to pay very close attention to details and warning signs, so you ensure that the test is completed and you will never be harmed in the same way twice unless you allow yourself to be. We leave the source to grow into our most authentic selves. Instead of being in pain that it happened to you, be thankful that you will never have to learn that lesson again and it is out of the way. Do not despise or hold anger towards your physical guides, they are not here to destroy you, they are a gift. One that has to be understood in order to be properly used as a tool.'

A line of three droplets rush down the right side of his facial structure, *'I never thought about it that way.'*

The Captain nods, *'Your fear of being alone prevents you from seeing the love in the situations. It stops you from noticing the Divine blessings in all things, but it does this the most when you need it the worst.'*

Time passes slowly by, I roll my neck to the side, releasing tension from my spinal cord.

A deep sigh is pushed from my lungs, directed towards the Captain, "This is taking a long time. Is there any way we can make this go any faster?"

She slowly motions her attention towards me, "Rushing their growth is not suggested. The process is already taking place at an intense speed due to the urgency of their situation.

Even though they are moving at a strong, steady pace, they have many lessons yet to learn."

I can feel a snarling growl being shot into the air around us, "Yeah, well they are not the ones who are trapped, I am!"

A soft smile rises against the right, corner of her mouth, "I understand that you are not comfortable and I apologize for your current situation. I really do. However, I was given a mission to help them into a higher state of understanding. I need to do my work with passion, not lust. This journey is a marathon, not a sprint. It is like a marriage. First, you have to be brave enough to meet yourself. Then you take it to the next step, figuring out how the communication between you and your authentic self is going to work. Once you know how to talk to yourself, you have to get to know every detail that makes you, you. Loving every imperfect picture and messy strand of hair. Once you find common ground and a sense of security in this new relationship, then it is time to devote yourself completely to this new way of life. When you realize that you are content and happy, that is when you start coming to the last hundred meters in the race. Even then, a sturdy speed is required to finish. You should be very proud of your friends, they are doing great."

I am unable to stop the words from pushing free from my mind, "They are not my friends! They mean nothing more to me than a victory, if they survive! Right now, they are completely worthless!"

The Captain does not even flinch under the deafening strum of my tone, "Well, I do not know what you want to call them, but they sure seem to care a lot about you. Enough to come save you, that is."

I can feel the backwards pull of my vision, "They have to come save me. How else would they complete the game?"

Her response sends a shiver across my chest, "You are not the game leader at this moment, Master Brutus is. They could leave without setting you free, but that never once even crossed their minds."

The sound of her voice melts from the surroundings as Austin tries to telepathically reach out to the Captain, 'I feel like something is deeply wrong inside of me, but I am unsure of what it is. Can you guide me in the right direction? Please.'

The Captain wastes no time melding their auras, 'I think that you are starting to experience the feeling of having 'lost' yourself. It became hidden under the patterns and thoughts of others. I am going to ask you a question. Based off of your answer, I will know if this is what you are fighting, okay?'

Austin nods slowly in agreement, his hesitation causes me to pick up on the uncertainty fueling his form.

The Captain does not allow an ounce of emotion to smear against her facial image, 'Who are you?'

Austin feels almost shocked by the simplicity of this theory, 'Who am I?'

Her thoughts do not waiver in confidence under his doubt, 'Yes. Who are you?'

He nods his head once in understanding, playing the words through his mind on repeat as he conjures up a reasonable response, *'Hmm. I suppose that this is a question that I could never really seem to answer.'*

A moment of silence passes slowly over the area before the Captain offers him words of comfort, 'Take your time. There is no wrong answer. This is just to help me understand how to better serve you.'

I can see Austin starting to fidget under the idea of not giving an answer yet.

It does not take him long to start producing some information, 'I am Austin James Parker. I love animals. My favorite color is blue. I like playing pool. I enjoy spending time with my friends and family, it is my happiest place to be.'

Another pause of his unsure mind coats the area, 'I think that is it. Well, it is all I can sort out of the mess that most people know as their brain, at this time. I am sorry if that information was not helpful.'

The Captain slowly gestures her head forward, *'Thank you for sharing this information with me. It is an honor to be in your circle of trust.'*

His response to her kind words is a small smile breaking against his lips at the notion of a compliment, something he is not used to receiving.

She releases a small chuckle around her thoughts, 'I am assuming you find the offer of affection and kindness from others to be unsettling?'

Austin finds himself attempting to untangle the clutter piling around his brain, 'To be honest, yes. It can be hard for me to accept even the smallest forms of affection from anyone. Even the cashier at the supermarket. Some people think it is just anxiety, but I am unsure. I wish it was something that was more socially acceptable, to show love to people who you are not in a romantic relationship with. That is why I turned to negative relationships because being in a bad relationship was better than not getting hugged or being able to hold someone's hand when you are sick or overwhelmed with joy. Being able to be content in another human's presence whether it is a romantic relationship or not, is a blessing that we all deserve to have in this world. A safe place, a space where we can escape without being torn apart by the same person who 'loves' you.'

The Captain smiles gently, '*Do not be hung up on the idea of changing everyone else. Apply the things you want to see in the world with your own life, others will want to help you make the dream a reality when they are able to see it in action. Embrace the side of you that sees the world differently, only when we see something from a new angle can we improve or alter something. Without a plan, the goal cannot be reached.*'

Austin nods in understanding, feeling a spark of curiosity ignite inside of his mind, '*Thank you for letting me know that. Really, you have no idea how much stress you just removed from my shoulders. I always was my own worst enemy when it came to freeing myself from the chains of the world. I was too afraid to make a difference, but now I feel like I cannot only take a stand, but I can be held sturdy. I have another question. I hope you can help with it. Can you please explain to me how I can be a better friend?*'

She releases a stream of air from her nasal passages, 'Are you questioning me in the view of love?'

Austin nods his head slightly, '*Yes. This sounds really strange, but I never want to come off as being weird when I show affection or care to my friends. Especially women, they always seem to mistake my kindness for me wanting something more than a friendship with them.*'

The weight of her skull falls forward slightly, '*I understand what you are trying to express. I, too had the same problem. The easiest way for me to get through it was this: if your intentions at the time are solely for the purpose of healing someone else then yes, give love freely to everyone and anyone.*

Imagine your friend, Luke and you are in the car driving in the rain and he is really afraid. It is okay for you to offer words of compassion, hold his hand, hug him, etc.

Giving love to others is one of the fastest ways to help them grow. Never be ashamed for loving someone. Love is the one thing in this world that strips away the illusions within and around us, giving us the ultimate freedom to become anything that we wish to be.

We will talk about this topic at a later time and if we do not get to it, your guides will help when the time is right.

Now, back to the question I asked you, 'who are you?'

Your answer shows me that you are currently in a very low vibration. Those things that you mentioned they are not who you are, but rather things that you either like or dislike.

Later, I will ask you that question again. Then we will compare the statements as a representation of your growth and self-identity.

If it slips both of our minds, do not fear, the universe has a greater plan. Always trust the natural flow and rhythm of the universe, every ounce of life that flows through her is magically beautiful.

Is this all making sense so far?'

Austin readjusts his posture while pulling his head into a small nod of agreement, *'I think so, yes. So far, I am understanding. It is just a lot of information. I don't think it all has had a chance to fully sink in, yet.'*

The Captain moves the placement of her hands from her lap to now drape over the structure of her knees, *'It is a lot of information. However, you are more than capable of retaining it all. Trust yourself, you can do this. You can do anything that you will allow yourself to do.*

I am glad everything so far is coming across clearly.

When you first start the journey of finding out who you are. It is vital to realize and accept that nobody else in this world should be able to convince you to think, feel or do something that does not feel right to you. Start over fresh in your mind, right now. Erase everything you think you know about yourself, life rules, everything. It is just gone.

Go through your life and replay interactions you have had with yourself and other people, but this time really keep your eyes open and gain perspective of how those same situations could have been handled in a better way.

It might be helpful if you ask yourself questions like, 'How could I have spoken clearer or more relaxed? How could I have handled that situation in a more loving and compassionate nature? What are some traits, emotions, thoughts or actions that I would like to improve on or add more of into my life?'

If your will to see a better version of yourself is stronger than your hold on who you currently are, you will always be given the information in some form on how to help you improve.

I want you to start that process right now and continue it for the rest of your life.

It will save you and other people from a great amount of sorrow in the future.'

He remains silent as her voice starts to fade from his mind.

I can see that he is starting to not resist the parts of himself that want to feel better. His urge to find a cure to this darkness that has been torturing him since he was only a boy is becoming so intense, he is willing to do anything.

CHAPTER NINETEEN:

It does not take long for our minds to be pulled towards Emily.

Once inside, we can hear thoughts being shot in every direction, 'What am I going to do to get Luke back? I have to get out of this situation. Maybe, this isn't the best way to find Luke. I am sure Austin and I could have come up with something better. I hate not knowing what is going to happen next. It is making me very uneasy.'

The water begins to unsettle under the frequency of her thoughts. A large bump in the path ahead causes the front of the boat to shoot up. Emily feels the right side of her body slam into the floor, a wave of dust splashes against her face.

The Captain waits longer than usual to offer a warm blanket of advice, 'Emily. Block everything else out besides the sound of my voice. Do you think that you can do that?'

Emily's reply is soft and weak as she attempts to re-position herself, 'Yes.'

The Captain nods once in understanding, *'Good. Now, what you are experiencing is your need for control of things and people. This falls into our 'human' side and is something we have to work on in order to grow.*

You are feeling this way because you are afraid. Scared of being vulnerable to the Divine.

To some people, they feel as though they wish they could just sit down at the kitchen table and have coffee with the higher power. If that is how you are feeling, I understand. I, too was there many times in my life until I took the time to try and understand, instead of assuming that I knew what was going on in the Divine's vibration. I decided to try and place myself there.

It really does make sense you know, why the Divine does not always mend our suffering for us. We came here with the intention of learning. Look at life as if it were a game. The lessons are just obstacles to make it both interactive and quick. Some lessons are on a positive frequency and others are on a lower.

However, it all should be approached with excitement and the desire to expand and grow. With that being said, we have to learn it on our own.

We know that we are in constant contact with the Divine and yet, so many people feel like it is a one-sided conversation.

You will think that way only until you understand it is like the two of you are speaking different languages.

You communicate through mental, emotional and verbal vibrations.

The Divine communicates with you telepathically, through numbers, lessons, blocks, people, angels, commercials, etc. Every single, little detail of your life is a sign in one direction or another, you just have to learn how to read it.

Once you understand how to properly receive the information, you will form trust.

This is about what you are not doing, not about what the Divine is not doing.'

Emily inhales a deep breath of calming, ocean air floating around our surroundings.

Upon her exhale her shoulders visibly loosen, *'Thank you. Truly, that helps me so much. You're right. This is something I have been struggling with for many years to understand. For a long time, I just assumed that the Divine forgot that I was even created. In reality, I just couldn't hear what was being spoken to me.'*

The Captain leans her weight forward slightly, *'You are welcome, Emily.'*

We retract our energy from Emily, giving her a chance to soak everything in as well as adapting to a new way of viewing herself and others.

I do not have very much alone time with the Captain. The whole time I have had this deep energy pulling me to talk to her. I have so many questions. Maybe, I cannot hear the answers or maybe, I am not as confident as I once thought I was.

My simmering thoughts are beginning to cool as something more important is suddenly being presented. It is Emily. Come on, let us go tune in on the excitement.

When I arrive, I am able to hear nothing other than silence. I cannot not help but to wonder what the Captain said to Emily to make her stop fitting this time.

The soft vibration of the Captain travels through the space, 'Are you feeling calmer now, Emily?'

She nods her head in a quick push of gratitude, *'Yes. Thank you.'*

The Captain swishes her weight between her hips, *'You are welcome. Do you understand what you were just experiencing?'*

Emily does not have to offer an actual response, her low vibration is enough of an answer for the Captain, who decides to speak instead, 'That is okay. You were experiencing what I like to refer to as emotional chaos. When this happens, your emotions will either cycle or cause you to remain helpless against your will in order to stop and prevent the severity of this lesson in the future. You are going to want to take back control of your own vibration.

You do this by turning all of your attention onto fixing this 'malfunction' and finding the information to overcome this within yourself.

When you are transitioning, remember you are the only one who is standing between you and who you want to be.'

I immediately feel the Captain pull us free from Emily's energy field.

The Captain turns her attention towards me, 'Are you learning anything by sitting in?'

I swallow roughly, nodding my head once in response.

She smiles softly in my direction, 'Good. I hope the information I have is able to assist you in many ways.'

The words I speak slice against the back of my mind, 'Are you implying that I am broken?'

She immediately places her right, index finger towards her sealed lips, *'Next time, can you please try to lower your thought frequency to a softer tone? I do not want to disturb their inner peace. They worked very hard so far and the battle is far from over.'*

I nod once in understanding. I hope my silence that I force, reminds her to address my last question.

She takes a deep breath of air, *'Thank you for being compassionate to their situation. To answer your previous question, no, my friend. I do not think you are broken. I think you are just stagnant.'*

The words she transfers spark a light inside of me with curiosity flowing under her theory. I can feel my soul sob with the realization of my true state.

A stale silence begins to fill the space, leaving her to her own thoughts and me with mine.

Thankfully, it does not take long for Emily to show signs of discomfort.

With all of our energy now connected, I feel a surge of excitement coursing through my form as I cannot help but to wonder what is next to be discovered about her and myself.

The moment we make connection with Emily, the sound of her voice blows through our minds, 'I am so worthless, what even is the point of me being here? I don't understand why some people are the way they are, why are they so mad at everything? I wonder why I like having my hair short and wearing male clothing? I wonder why the guy at the coffee shop the day we were planning our road trip left without paying his tab. I wonder—'

Emily is cut off by her own wrongdoing as a clash of water slams into the left side of the boat causing her body to fly backwards.

She cracks the back of her head roughly against the wooden panels behind her form, "Ouch! I really wish that would stop happening!"

The Captain nods once in understanding with her current situation, *'Once you figure out how to control your thoughts, you will master the world around you. Now, to help with the bigger problem, let's start somewhere else. You are learning non-judgement of yourself and other people. It is very common to be judgmental of something you have never been through.*

However, it is just as easy to judge others for going through the same thing as well.

When you start down the journey of accepting yourself in the sense of understanding completely who you are and where you are going. Who you end up is all based off of your vibration. In order to get there, you have to allow yourself to release all of your own and others baggage.

Think of yourself for a moment, you go out into the sun and your skin turns red, right? Are you still the same person as you were when you came outside only hours before?'

Emily raises her right hand towards her facial structure,

removing a strand of her hair that has fallen into a place of annoyance.

She hopes this gives her a moment to ensure she is in full understanding of the question, *'Well, yes. Of course.'*

The Captain nods slowly, *'Then why would you judge someone else for something that does not really matter? If you are no different if you are white or red, then there is no difference between you and anyone else.*

The things you currently think matter, the money, the fame, the women, the men, the cars, jobs, your house, jealousy, anger, fear, revenge, etc. These things that you think matter so much to you in this moment, will one day be nothing more than a thing for pleasure or a part of the past.

You will understand a greater sense of 'oneness' once we open your Divine energy port, but we are not there yet.

In the meantime, to help with all of the negative effects of judgement that can spill out onto yourself and others, try to walk into every situation with an open mind and a positive, high vibration.

If you find after giving it a fair chance that something is just not right with a person or a situation then there is no law that says you have to remain around or accept the negative energy towards yourself or someone else. You always have a choice to walk away from anything that is mentally, emotionally, spiritually or physically harmful. That is your power, you are in control of what you are allowing to stay and what you are not. Once you find that you do not want something then you may hold an opinion. Do not carry associations of one person to another, but if signs start showing up and you are not unintentionally creating them based off past trauma then yes, trust it.

Remain calm by accepting this: You cannot change or predict how someone will react to you until you try. If you get a bad feeling, leave. Trust yourself enough to have learned from past lessons, but do not fool yourself by preventing future blessings.

Remember, only when you fully allow yourself to just be, is the fastest and most effective way to gain control over this fear.'

Emily nods quickly, *'Thank you for helping me. You have no idea how many times I tried to defeat these things on my own with no success. To be honest, I did not even realize some of these things existed inside of me until now.'*

The Captain dips her head forward once, *'Yet, there is still so much to learn. This is only the beginning.'*

Emily tilts her head to the left as if it helps her grab a hold of her thoughts, *'Will the rest of the journey help me grow as well?'*

The Captain cannot help but to release a sincere chuckle, *'Every step of the way.'*

CHAPTER TWENTY:

My mind buzzes with life under the Captain's movements.

I watch her pull her form into a full stance, making her way over towards the back wall by the table.

It does not take her long to turn back around and once again find her comfort in a crisscrossed, seated position.

Her voice pounds against my ear drums, "Austin, Emily. Please, once again hold out your hands and we will transfer the stones."

Both of my pawns act instantly to her vocal commands.

They can feel a tingling sensation against their palms as she places a lemon quartz in their grasp, "Okay, you may now replace your hands into their previous positions. This energy sphere is yellow in hue and is the placement of a lot of your internal work. You can use this stone just as you have with the others. When something comes up, let me know and I will try my best to assist in any way that I can."

They adjust themselves, trying to find a perfect placement.

I can feel my mind pulling away from them and onto myself. It does not take long for my daydream to turn into a nightmare.

Thoughts explode against my mind in a child-like destruction, 'I wonder if they are ever going to get through this? They are my only hope for survival. I have to get out of here and take back my game to prove to Master Brutus that I am not a complete failure.'

The rhythm of my tone is shattered by a woman's voice entering from the left, 'Is that really the only reason you are here? I was hoping it was so you could support their growth and that you could take a few things from this yourself. Even if you are not yet ready to part with old ways, it never hurts to learn something new.'

I can feel my mind automatically shoot back a short phrase of agreement, 'You are right, I will try harder.'

A gentle smile rises to her mouth in my direction before she shifts her focus onto Austin and Emily.

This encounter with the Captain has left me feeling very out of touch with my usual self. It would seem that maybe there is more to me than what I have become.

A moment of silence gives my brain a chance to process the last ten minutes with clarity, 'What the hell is happening to me?'

My self-evaluation is cut short by Austin beginning to show signs of needing help. We waste no time merging our minds with his.

His thoughts are flowing at a rapid pace, 'I don't understand why I am having such a hard time fully transitioning. I know what I have to do, I just can't seem to put it into action. I guess, that is just because I am only human, huh?'

The Captain can feel the floorboards beneath their weight beginning to shake from the energy currents being emitted from his mind.

She does not allow the negative energy to torture him any longer, 'You feel powerless. It is a very common blockade to run into when you start doing maintenance on yourself. May I ask you a question?'

I can hear the static shock run along his mind, 'Yes, of course. Anything.'

The Captain nods once in appreciation, *'In the beginning of your journey with me, when we talked about making choices for ourselves as if we were making them for our loved one. If the person, who you thought of was in the same situation as you are right now. What would you tell them?'*

Austin feels his head fall back slightly as he thinks the question over, *'That they should allow the transition to take over every inch of their life because they deserve happiness. They deserve the hope of being able to spread love to themselves and others. We all want to be the best version of ourselves mind, body and soul. If you have found a way to create peace within yourself, why not take it? Take the chance. What is the worst thing that could happen? You stay exactly how you are right now. This could propel you into being the greatest construction of you, but if you, are not a good enough reason in your mind yet to make this change, please know that this is not just about you. It is for everyone you come in contact with. You have two options every day, spread fear or love. I do not know about you, but I would rather make people feel good. This growth in you, is about so much more than just you.'*

The Captain tries to hold back a growing grin, *'I think you gave yourself very good advice. You should listen to yourself more, Austin. Trust your soul, it has been around for a very long time. You are ready for this. When it gets tough, re-evaluate the plan, but never stop searching for the goal. You are already getting stronger. I am so proud of you.'*

He can feel the connection between them beginning to fade away as he releases a cracked vibration, 'Thank you.'

The Captain and I watch him in silence for the next three hours. We pay attention to every wince, squint, adjustment and physical reaction he shows during the battle within himself that he must face.

Finally, after the long stretch of empty air, words break into the silence from Austin, "Help, please."

The Captain melts her energy into his, 'Make sure you stop your thoughts again for a while and relax your mind. Once you reach a higher vibration inside of your brain's activity, we will discuss what was causing you such great pain. You are not alone through this, I am here. I just need you to be calm, so I can assist you in the best way possible.'

He nods his head slowly, inhaling a deep breath before regaining control of his mind.

It does not take long for Austin to get the upper hand, 'Okay, I am ready. Thank you for waiting.'

The Captain nods gently, *'What is it that you need help with, Austin?'*

I can hear him swallow the fear from here, 'I was taking your advice. It was going really well. So far, I feel like I have made many upgrades since we spoke last, but one came up and I just can't figure out how to get through it.'

She pushes her weight to the right, *'What is it that you are unable to get through?'*

His head tips down slightly in shame, *'Addictions. I have relied on something else to make me happy for so long. I am unsure how to transition into a life without it. However, I am aware that in this current time that I do not have nor need it. Yet, I live in a constant state of fear that makes me think, 'What if I need it in the future?''*

The Captain smiles gently, *'I understand what you are going through—"*

Before the Captain has a chance to respond, Austin releases a harsh stream of words, 'Oh yeah? How do you know that?'

She does not allow more than a second of silence to pass, 'I was an addict, too.'

We can see his eyes reacting to her words by rocketing from side to side underneath his lids, 'You? Really? You seem so happy. I would have never guessed that.'

An uncontrollable laugh runs against the back of her throat, *'Yes, you are correct. I am very happy. Thank you. I needed it at one point in my life, but that does not mean that I want to continue to abuse it.*

Right here, right now, in this moment, you are completely safe. The only thing that is against you, is you. In this moment, there is nothing that you need to escape from. The easiest way to overcome an addiction is to look inside of yourself while in meditation. You have to find the root cause of what is going on. Do not stop evaluating the issue of your addiction until you are at peace. It is different for everyone, but whatever it is, the initial reason is fear.

Once you find the core, it will be easier for you to cut the mental, emotional and physical ties with the substance.

This will take you to the transitioning phase which includes breaking the attachment on a physical level by slowing cutting down and replacing it with something you love just as much as you feared letting go of your addiction. This practice will help reset your mind to go in a different direction allowing you the power to break free from your negative cycle of thoughts.

When going through this shift, there is something I want you to remember:

When you are an addict, you still have bad days. Things still go wrong, your vibration and mindset can and will remain low. You still have money trouble, you still have the job you hate, you still are dealing with all of the things you are trying to run from. They are just amplifying in strength when you try to silence them under a sheet of alcohol and drugs. It does not weaken your battles, it only fuels them.'

Austin smiles as a tear runs down the left side of his facial structure, *'Thank you. I will start working on that immediately.'*

The Captain smirks, *'Remember, Austin. If you continue to do things that hurt you, that teaches others that they can hurt you as well. Once you stop hurting yourself with addictions, your past, your diet, your mind, you will regain trust within yourself.*

How can you trust yourself fully when you are the person you are fighting?

Win the battle, the war has already been won. All you have to do is trust you can do this.'

CHAPTER TWENTY-ONE:

Austin's mind barely has any time at all to calm down before we are being yanked in the direction of Emily.

Her eyes are being held tightly shut as a soft whine is released from her lungs.

Before I have a chance to fully grasp the event that just ended with Austin. I can feel myself being dragged into another adventure.

The emotional and mental discomfort has already passed by the time we enter her thoughts.

The Captain lets Emily know we are here by transferring information in a soft tone, 'What are you experiencing?'

A nervous laugh is shot in our direction, 'I was just sitting here thinking about my life and it made me realize that maybe, I am not as good of a person as I once thought I was. I feel almost afraid of myself and my thoughts, my emotions and my actions. They frighten me.'

The Captain raises her vibration, sending the frequency to Emily in the form of thoughts, 'I understand the realization and all that you are feeling. I was there at one point as well.
Remember, when you were in world four and you learned the lesson about deflection?'

Emily struggles to piece together an answer, 'Yes, why?'

The Captain attempts to make her tone even more appealing, 'Right now, you are dealing with deflection that people on Earth associate with 'hell'. With that being said, this journey will awaken your mind and force you to face any 'demons' that might come up to the surface.

These battles that you are facing should be looked at as learning, not trauma.

Right now, you are in between your soul and your ego.

The ego is put inside of you from a very young age as a shield of protection or known to some as being on 'autopilot'.

It can be used to help numb the initial pain of a traumatic event to aid you in a better coping and understanding of that lesson.

However, it does come with a few side-effects, the biggest one is lowering your vibration to a severe depth, one that is not easy to just walk out of. If comes with a fight, that is what you are up against right now.

I am going to share with you some characteristics of both, so it can help you in distinguishing between them.

Soul:

- *Captivated by miracles.*
- *Understanding of others and your own human side.*
- *Never gives up.*
- *Always relaxed.*
- *Allows nature to help guide your way.*
- *Asks others how you can better serve them.*
- *Learns from past mistakes.*
- *Knows we are all equal, we are all one.*
- *No desires.*
- *Always fulfilled.*
- *Selfless.*
- *Does not allow others to harm you.*
- *Keeps promises.*
- *Knows you are very loved and worthy.*
- *Let's go of things that no longer serve you.*
- *Does not allow other vibrations to affect you.*
- *Remains clean and organized in life, mind and soul.*
- *Positive and peaceful reactions to people and situations.*
- *Full faith in ourselves.*

- *Looks inward for advice.*
- *Bliss.*
- *Happiness.*
- *Is in the moment.*
- *Balanced non-attachment.*
- *Balanced self-care.*
- *Positive thoughts.*
- *Knows life is a classroom and a paradise entangled into one.*
- *Positive emotions.*
- *Contentment.*
- *Aids you in seeking the truth.*
- *Truthful.*
- *Transparent.*
- *Faithful.*
- *Acknowledges others suffering.*
- *Talks about happiness, ideas, life and miracles.*
- *Acceptance.*
- *Apologizes.*
- *Blames ourselves when a mistake is made.*
- *Wants a soul attraction.*
- *Empathy.*
- *Allows the Divine to be in control.*
- *Does not require closure.*
- *Respectful to all life.*
- *Does not crave acknowledgement.*
- *Balanced self-love.*
- *Mental clarity.*
- *Full faith in the Divine.*
- *Love.*
- *Child-like.*
- *Forgiveness.*
- *Healing.*
- *Proper use of 'power'.*
- *Excitement.*
- *Harmony.*
- *Peace.*
- *Shameless.*

- *Patience.*
- *Limitless.*
- *Waits for others to express themselves.*
- *Accepts that you make mistakes.*
- *Knows Earth's limitations do not define you.*
- *Is our connection to the Divine.*
- *Is connected to our authentic self.*
- *Believes in magic.*
- *Giving.*
- *Looks for patterns in people.*
- *You vs. You.*
- *Fearless.*

Ego:

- *You vs. The world.*
- *Wants to fight.*
- *Falls for words and actions of others.*
- *Stealing.*
- *Feeling 'mucky'.*
- *Lack of faith in ourselves.*
- *Looks outward for advice.*
- *Empty.*
- *Interrupt others.*
- *Mental illness.*
- *Greed.*
- *Not knowing your authentic self.*
- *Secretive.*
- *Selfish.*
- *Lack of empathy.*
- *Purposely doing the wrong thing after being told.*
- *Considers yourself to be only a 'human'.*
- *Makes you old inside and out.*
- *Steals the miracles of life.*
- *Childishness.*
- *Thinks you are better than someone else.*
- *Not feeling close to the Divine.*

- *Needs closure.*
- *Does not allow you to control your own thoughts, emotions or actions. Doing things without thinking first.*
- *Mistaken idea of self-love.*
- *Demands to be heard.*
- *Fear.*
- *Ignoring someone.*
- *Negative thoughts, emotions and actions.*
- *Makes you think that you are unworthy.*
- *Allows others to treat you poorly.*
- *Thinks you need to use vulgar, crude words or sarcasm to better express yourself.*
- *Makes you unorganized and unclean.*
- *Stubborn.*
- *Sadness.*
- *Suffering.*
- *Holds grudges.*
- *Negative reactions to situations and people in everyday life.*
- *Starting, believing or participating in rumors.*
- *Hanging onto the past.*
- *Not being able to keep promises to yourself or others.*
- *Violence.*
- *Stress.*
- *Power.*
- *Blames others for problems in your life or mistakes you have made.*
- *Manipulation.*
- *Cheating.*
- *Lying.*
- *Disconnected from reality.*
- *Thinks life is hard or overwhelming.*
- *Judgmental.*
- *Physical attractions.*
- *Being unteachable.*
- *Abuses other people's kindness.*
- *Impatient.*
- *Needs to be in control.*

- *Tries to play the Divine's role with things by forcing situations such as friends, partners, jobs, etc.*
- *Thinks you are always right.*
- *Attachment to people, thoughts, emotions or memories.*
- *Lack of self-care.*
- *Jealously.*
- *Anger.*
- *Shame.*
- *Guilt.*
- *Lack of faith in the Divine.*
- *Limitations.*
- *Abusive behaviors: mental, emotional and physical.*
- *Self-harm.*
- *Desire.*
- *Addictions.*

I know that this is a lot of information to take in all at once. Just try to remember as many of them on the soul side for right now.

These are not the full lists of either side, I just wanted to give you as many examples as possible to help you understand on a deeper level what you are dealing with right now.

This might seem overwhelming, but the easiest way to determine a soul thought, emotion or action from an ego trait is by paying attention to the energy you are receiving.

If it lowers your vibration, hurts you or another living creature mentally, physically or emotionally, that is your ego.

It will come up, a lot. Sometimes it will it be worse than others. It all depends on what you have been through, but we all have this battle to face to some degree or another.

When it will not stop, it wants your attention. Do not run, try to understand what is causing you the discomfort, so you can solve it and prevent this battle from peeking at another point in your life.

A great tip here is to know if you solved the problem or if you need to keep looking for a better solution by remembering this: if it still hurts, keep searching.

When the battle is over and the base of the issue is removed, the next part of your job is transitioning.

Make sure you give yourself more than enough room to grow and in moments when you feel like you do not deserve this switch remember, all the pain you endured in your life to get to this moment. You have more than earned it.'

CHAPTER TWENTY-TWO:

I can feel the moment nagging at my attention as anxiety crawls up the back of my throat due to this taking much longer than I originally assumed.

The weight of my head falls to the right in annoyance towards the Captain, who begins to show signs of movement.

She shifts her mass between the sides of her hips, "Okay, we are going to switch stones again. Make sure you only free yourself from your current state long enough to make the transfer. Then you will be on your own until assistance is needed or it is time to move on to the next level. Please, hold out your hands. Thank you."

My pawns do not hesitate when following the Captain's orders, I feel a shot of emotion exploding inside of my chest at the sight.

The words in my mind take an unexpected, dark shift, 'That is humorous. I see they are listening to her and not me. They have never been so obedient to me. What makes her so great?'

The realization that my thoughts on this plane are not private causes me to desperately regain control of myself, just in time to see the Captain explaining a little bit more about the next area that they are moving onto.

Before fully allowing my attention to consume her, my subconscious whispers, 'We have to do better at controlling the conscious part of our mind.'

The structure of my voice begins to fade as the Captain's enters, 'This next energy filter is for the heart. Its color is green and the crystal in your hand is a rose quartz. This energy portal will unleash love onto yourself and others unconditionally when properly balanced. When you are exploring this area of yourself, the easiest thing to do is ensure the balance of love between yourself and others is equal. I will be right here if you need any help."

Thankfully for me, I do not have to wait long in a realm of my own, internal suffering.

Austin begins to show signs of panic almost ten Earth minutes into the session.

The Captain and I nearly jump at the sight.

The moment our souls connect, I feel an intense emptiness beginning to build inside of myself. Once of which I assumed I would never feel again, guilt.

The Captain does not give his emotions the approval of tormenting him any longer, 'What are you fighting?'

A loud sniff of his clogged airway pounds against our ears as he tries to hold in a flood of tears, 'I just—I guess, I get really frustrated with myself because my pain causes harm to others and myself. Sometimes, when I hear people complaining about their situations, it makes me very upset because what I went through was so much worse than what they did. Yet, I released mine or tried to, at least. These people allow the smallest things to stop them. I just do not get it. I lack compassion for those who have had it easier than me. It can make me moody, disconnected, lonely and judgmental, but it upsets me more than anything because I know those thoughts and feelings are not who I really am. I want nothing more than to be freed of this suffering.'

The Captain nods once in understanding, 'At one point, I found myself staring into the same mirror. I do sympathize with your discomfort.

The best way for me to properly learn how to handle the human side of others as well as myself was to think back to the bigger picture of why we are here which is to learn.

Your life is perfectly tailored to your lessons and the severity of those lessons all depend on what level you are at in your education and how gracefully you decide to follow your path.

Anyone who you look at with an 'easier' life than you, do not envy them.

Their life is to only learn so much at this time, in this body, in this dimension. At one point, you were them and one day, they will be you.

Offer them as much help as you can now, so when they do get to the level you are at, their suffering might not be so painful.

I want you to take a minute and play as much of your life as you can remember through your mind from the age of nine, until now. While you are doing this, really allow every clip to fully set in. Emotions, thoughts, actions and every other little detail.

Tell me when you are done.'

Austin inhales a deep breath of the cleansing air, *'I can't remember many things from my past. Doctors assume I purposely blocked them to avoid pain, but what I can recall, I reviewed.'*

The Captain sits up straighter, raising the vibration of her tone, *'Your memories should start coming back when this energy port becomes balanced.*

After you review your life events, I would also like you to keep everyone who hurt you in mind.

Now, tell me which person from your past would you want to give your life to?'

Austin does not allow more than two seconds to pass in silence, 'None. I wouldn't wish my life on anyone, not even the person who hurt me the most.'

The Captain's tone informs me that she is pleased with his response, 'Then why would you want someone else to have a worse version of their own? Trust the process of a higher power. You can only do your part and in some cases, 'your part' is very slim, but that does not mean that it is not the most important piece.'

He allows her words to sink into the structure of his mind, 'Can I ask you a question? I am unsure if it has to do with this energy wheel or not.'

The Captain responds in relief at the interest he is showing, 'Of course. Ask anything you wish, my friend.'

Austin nods his head once in an uncontrollable act of gratitude, *'I have an issue with allowing people to be close to me or letting them and myself exchange unconditional love. I do not like this about myself, how do I change it?'*

The Captain nods slowly as she plays the question through her mind twice, *'This is very normal when dealing with this area of the body.*

You are afraid of being hurt. The easiest way to overcome this is by accepting that you have no control over someone else.

This fear does not have anything to do with other people, it only involves you. You have to trust yourself enough to know that if signs do come up, you will act accordingly to the situation. Walk into every relationship from this moment on with unconditional love.

If they do something minor, express your feelings. If it still does not change then you can evaluate from there.

If they leave, do not be disheartened. Take a deep breath and remind yourself that there is someone out there, who will make you realize that magic does exist.

One of the most effective ways to ensure that your love does not overwhelm you or the other person is by setting up time together as well as apart. Loving someone should aid their mental, emotional, spiritual and physical well-being.

Do not allow your love to blind you from seeing the pain and do not allow your fear to keep you from seeing the love.

Live by this simple structure and love will never be something you fear again.

Love makes you strong, fear implies you need more love.
The society on Earth tries to convince us that it is the other way around.
Do not listen to them, trust yourself.'

Austin tilts his head to the right, *'Is that why you left Earth?'*

The Captain exhales loudly, *'I could not live in a world without love, so I decided to create my own.'*

CHAPTER TWENTY-THREE:

Now that Austin has been saved from one battle, he silently moves onto the next.

This leaves me alone with my thoughts. My mind keeps replaying the last speech given by the Captain as well as her answer to Austin's question.

The things she says, they are starting to make more sense to me.

I just feel like I need a little more time to evaluate them further.

The Captain does not appear to be disturbed by my doubtful thinking. In fact, she does not even jump to her own defense. Instead, she moves onto the next task as Emily begins showing symptoms of being uncomfortable.

The Captain tilts her head to the left, admiring her from a different angle, *'Emily, is everything okay?'*

Shrugged shoulders are the only response she receives.

The Captain does not leave her alone with her pain, she only remains silent giving Emily room to process.

It does not take long for words to begin leaking from the faucet of her mind, 'I don't know. I guess, a big problem I have always, secretly held onto is being jealous of other people for the things they have. I didn't have a lot of stuff in my life growing up the way I did. I never honestly admitted to myself how much it bothered me until now. I do not like having these emotions or thoughts. How can I reset it to something nicer?'

The Captain does not seem surprised by her confession, 'Why are you feeling jealous? Is it because you really want those things or is it that you are simply trying to fill something inside of yourself since you feel empty?'

The words spill from her mind, 'Yes! How do you know that?'

The Captain cannot help but to release a small chuckle, *'Yes? Which one? I had to go through similar events.'*

Emily's cheeks burn red under the acknowledgement of what she had just done, *'I'm sorry. The one about feeling alone or empty. I always thought having all the money, friends and things I ever wanted would finally fill that void that I have been so desperately trying to cover since I was younger.'*

The Captain exhales briefly, *'Jealous is normally associated with a lack of something. We normally feel the intensity of this emotion when we allow the outside opinions of others to make us feel like something is wrong with us because we do not have something that they think we should. We try to 'buy' or force ourselves to fit into a negative vibration rather than breaking free from it.*
Do you truly believe that those things will make you happier?'

She releases a long breath of emotion, *'No. If anything, right now, at this point in my life they would make me feel more alone.'*

The Captain nods her head in understanding, *'Then you are already halfway there. Is it alright if I offer you some advice that I was given by my teacher? I feel certain that it will aid you in this situation and hopefully many more in the future.'*

Emily's thoughts quietly break through the area in a soft manner, 'Yes, please.'

The Captain smiles, hoping to bring her a sense of comfort by gently raising her vibration, *'People only want to know enough about you to make a bad judgement. They hear what they want to hear, see what they want to see and you will only be what they will allow you to be. This whole time, you thought you were trapped by their opinions, but only now do you realize you have been freed.'*

CHAPTER TWENTY-FOUR:

The Captain fiddles with the two, marble, white and light blue stones in each of her palms.

It does not take her long to interrupt the silence in the room, "If you both are ready, we can move onto the next energy point."

She receives the silent response of them both nodding their heads while extending their dominate hand to make the switch.

The Captain wastes no time to replace the piece, "This is an aquamarine stone and the hue associated with this energy sphere is blue. Again, if something comes up, you know the drill."

Five minutes into the pawns resetting back into their thoughts, Austin starts to show signs of intense frustration.

The Captain is already intertwining us with him.

She attempts to find a more comfortable position to sit in, *'Austin, is everything alright?'*

A nervous laugh starts playing through his mind, 'Yes, sorry. These things are all just pooping up like crazy. I feel like I am barely able to get over one before I am faced with something new.'

The Captain smirks in a soothing manner, *'That is a good sign. It means you are ready to let these things go and move on.'*

Austin pushes his head forward once in an unsure understanding.

She continues to allow her voice to occupy the space, 'What is it that is causing you to be so disheartened?'

Austin pushes all of his weight towards her in a nervous manner, *'I mean, it's not really a secret or anything and it came up as soon as you changed out the rocks. I have a fear of public speaking. Then, of course that one thought causes a whole line of thoughts to follow that are backing that statement up.*

After the thoughts start to get jumbled and become overwhelming, my brain will play out different scenarios through my head. I try to perfect and fix them to better fit what I want to happen, but in the moment of having the situation appear in my mind, I always freeze which forces me to resort to my old habits.'

The Captain exhales deeply allowing every drop of air to be felt on her upper lip as it exits her form, *'That is a very generalized fear which can be started and grows in different situations, for many reasons. You are afraid of what other people think of you. You are fearful that you might say the wrong thing or mess up. The reason you are having these thoughts is due to something deeper. Once you find the main reason you are feeling this way, you can then tackle the core in one sweep.*

The going over scenarios in your mind is a good thing, but you have to make sure you are building these things while you are in a high vibration. When you are visualizing, you use a lot of different emotions. To your brain, it feels real. You are reacting to the situation based off what you are essentially 'wishing' would happen and your passion makes that hope a reality.

This will all get easier, you are doing great so far, keep it up! You should be very proud of yourself.

When it comes to the other battle you mentioned, having an overactive mind.

This quality can either be looked at as a good or bad thing. However, it is all thankfully up to you based on how you want to experience the situation.

Being an overthinker will always keep your imagination strong. Informing you that what you think will result in a state of dreaming allows you to choose if it is going to be built around fear or love.

The two areas that you are working with are not really problems that still need to be addressed, we are just polishing up what you have already learned.'

CHAPTER TWENTY-FIVE:

With our minds now no longer connected to Austin, the staleness of the air is starting to get on my nerves. It is almost as if I can feel it beneath my skin.

A deep breath of relaxation is pulled from my lungs. Thankfully, something appears to be going on with Emily, giving me a break from trying to understand my own mind by entering hers.

Emily immediately picks up on our energetic presence, 'I have always had an issue with explaining and expressing myself in situations.

In these times of empty mindedness, it would make sense to replace what I couldn't express with something I could explain in my mind.

I never mean to do it in a deceiving manner, but rather help someone else understand a bigger picture of what I am trying to say when my vocal cords fail me with their lack of connection to my brain.

I think it was a coping method to make myself not have to admit that I had a period of time in my life with severe long and short-term memory loss from trauma and unhealthy healing methods.

Most people have great stories to tell and I have no mental representation of things that happened to me, especially the good things.

Do you know why this is occurring or at least how I can fix it?'

The Captain nods her head slowly as if her connection with the situation is more personal than even Emily knows, *'Yes, I have an idea. However, like I have said before, I can give you a general direction, but if what I say does not completely take away the pain then there is something deeper going on that you will need to look into. You do this by watching and evaluating your own patterns, seeing how you react to certain situations. In that moment of understanding why you are acting a certain way is when you have the ability to make progress in a different direction. Once the core is located, I can assist you further at that point.*

When it comes to your current situation, I think it is a mixture of still caring about how you look to other people and feeling like the life you experienced stole your hope for a better tomorrow.

However, you fail to see the beauty in the situation. You might have started this journey in the dark, but due to the work you are putting into yourself right now, the future is going to be brighter than you ever could have imagined.

Whatever it is that is causing you to be deceitful, do not allow that fear to create more discomfort in the long run because you are too afraid to be honest.

Use all of those thoughts to build the best adventure for your future and projects that you are working on in your everyday life.

The things you speak are not really for you. The things you say are there to help others understand you better, those words have a frequency which can be felt on some level of sensitivity. Negative vibrations are easy to pick up on. Understand the power of your ability to express things vocally, but only use this release of energy in a positive, loving, honest and accepting manner.

Having this mindset will help to reprogram you to pause and look over yourself before just freely expressing every thought that passes through your head. Once you master this technique with your thoughts, you will be able to gain the upper hand over feelings, words and actions.

Once all four battles are won, the past way of handling situations that bring up this defensive manner will be demolished and you will find peace in this area of your soul.'

CHAPTER TWENTY-SIX:

The Captain pulls herself into a firm stance, advancing quickly over to the table.

I watch her hands move softly against the top, the echoing pound of some rocks knocking against the wooden flesh startles me slightly.

Yet, she remains calm, walking back towards my mortals with four items in her hands.

It does not take her long to get resettled in her spot, "Austin. Emily. We are moving onto the next area now. If you both are ready, that is."

The only response she receives is a rhythmic motion of nodding heads and extended palms, waiting for the switch to be made.

A fast glimpse of a half-smile melting against her lips comes into view, "Good. You guys are really doing great. I am extremely proud of you so far and you should be even more proud of yourselves. I know that right here, in the moment, you are not able to see many, if any results, but I want you both to know that the steps you have taken are not insignificant at all. They are only going to get better every single day.

The next area of energy is your soul's window.

When you were born, this energy portal was open and life was great.

At some point, I do not know when, it is different for everyone, but something happened that made your mind go into *'autopilot'*. When that happened, your ego took control.

This is only supposed to be used as a temporary shield of protection while you sort things out that caused you to be put into this mindset in the first place. Then you are supposed to pull yourself back out of it. Once you are out, you restore your life back to your original functioning habits. When your ego takes control, your soul's window closes as you have to look inward in order to solve the problem. When you are ready to re-awaken this part of yourself and allow your soul to take over your thoughts, emotions and actions once again, just nod your heads. I will show you how to see.

First, I must inform you of something. When you look at things from your soul, they change for the better. It is a beautiful catastrophe and I feel blessed every moment that I get to be here and learn.

Thank you, both of you for allowing me to be a part of your journey. It has been an honor this far."

They both nod their head twice. Silence falls heavily over the room as the trade of rocks in being made.

My pawns allow their dominate hand to return to a resting placement on their lap.

Hardly any time passes before Austin starts showing physical symptoms of inner chaos such as mild sweating and an abnormal heartbeat. The two mix together with a shot of chest pain and shortness of breath.

His eyes squint tightly together as sharp pain runs against his neck and jaw line.

The world around him begins to react immediately to his energy, feeling the jerking movements of the molecules around them rocking the boat from right to left.

The Captain exhales a long, slow breath before merging

her mind with his.

I follow close behind, not wanting to miss a single second.

Both of my palms glide towards my ears to attempt to block out the thoughts that are firing against his mind, 'I am really scared. I'm not exactly sure what is going on. I feel like I just want to run away. I don't know to where, I just want to run.'

The Captain nods her head quickly, *'If I could snap my fingers and grant you one wish right now that would ease this tension to something more bearable. What would you desire the most?'*

Austin releases a harsh breath from his parted lips, *'Honestly, I would want to be able to transition from who I was when I walked in that door, to who I truly want to be in every aspect of my life, without fearing that everything is going to fall apart when I do make the switch. I just want to be happy. I no longer wish to suffer from the things that I am not battling today. I want to be free.'*

The Captain offers him words of a warming comfort, 'The good news is, I do not have to be a genie to help make this wish come true.

All you have to do is go with the flow and leave the rest up to the Divine. Trust the blessings.'

Austin wastes no time speaking the next line, 'No offense, but how am I supposed to trust someone I can't talk directly to? I have no idea what is going on in the Divine's mind. If I could have communication, my trust would grow immensely.'

The Captain fails at attempting to hold back a small chuckle, *'The Divine does speak to you, all the time. All you have to do is learn the language. It is simple, if you ask and all signs point towards no, then forgive yourself for almost accepting something less than what you deserve and open yourself up to what the Divine and your higher self knows that you need the most.*

If the signs are pointing towards yes, then enjoy every single moment of pure love you are given.

For example:

If you ask the Divine to help you find happiness.

You might think money is your key to this feeling, but maybe it is love.

If you spend all of your focus on trying to get money to make you happy, you could miss out on the true source of your joy. Then one day, in the future you would realize that after you got this money, you still felt sad and then what are you going to do? Complain to the Divine that you are not happy.

Yet, you could have been happy the entire time while you were getting your money, if you would have just left an open mind to what would bring you this inner bliss, instead of ignoring it for something that will only make you feel more empty than whole if you do not have the right circumstances or positive motives to spend it on.

Learn the language by staying receptive to all paths that might take you to your main goal.

The more you notice and appreciate the Divine signs and blessings, the more you will see them throughout every step of your journey.

Have some faith, you are safe. You always were, whether you knew it or not. This connection will become stronger and bolder when we work on this energy point.'

A few moments of silence runs across the area before a crackling static of words are emitted from Austin's mind, 'This might come off as an odd question, but I was wondering if you could tell me why my memory is so poor. I sort of always noticed it but I guess, I brushed it off as being normal, yet here in this room, I feel like it is something I need to address and solve, but I am unsure how.'

The Captain tilts her head to the right, *'What kind of things do you find yourself forgetting? Good things, bad things, sort term or long?'*

Austin allows himself time to sit inside of his thoughts, 'Both short and long. Some bad, but mostly good things. It is weird, but ever since I walked in here it seems like I am losing sight of everything about me and my life before I met you. It's a slow process, but I can feel it all starting to just fade away. What does this mean?'

The Captain readjusts her hands to now rest in a relaxed sway against her knees, *'It is nothing that you need to worry yourself with, that is completely normal. You went through the trauma, learned the lesson and as you get to the source of your discomfort, the nagging memories will vanish as they are no longer needed, you have recovered.*

Like I said before, everything will change for the positive, just go with the flow of this new life, new you, new love and allow new blessings to reach every inch of your existence.

You have earned every ounce of happiness, do not be afraid. You are free. All you have to do is be brave enough to walk out of the cage, the door is open.'

CHAPTER TWENTY-SEVEN:

My mind is not allowed much time to get lost in itself as my attention flickers against Emily.

I am not even the slightest bit surprised to see that the Captain is already investigating the case.

Emily's mind is being bombarded by overwhelming questions, 'Why did I have to go through what I went through in my life? Is there really a bigger picture? Why isn't anything connecting? I feel so jumbled, I can't even sort where one thought begins and another ends. This all sounds too easy, too good to be true. Maybe, it is all too good to be true. Maybe, I am foolish for trying to think I could actually overcome these battles.'

Emily feels the violent shaking of the rickety boards being the only thing between them and a tornado of rapid waves.

When she realizes that she is losing control of her physical form, it causes thoughts to shoot through her mind, 'I have no idea what is wrong with me, this is so simple. Why am I torturing myself like this?'

The Captain breaks the pattern of her shadowy thoughts by relaying information in a light tone, 'The things that you are currently feeling are perfectly normal. Do not allow them to stir up negative feelings of doubt or over evaluation. When you allow the universe room to work its magic, all the answers will be given at the right time and the right place. If you cannot find the lesson in a situation then there are still things that need to be discovered about it. Go back through your mind and follow the pain, it will lead you to the places inside of yourself that have the heaviest rain.

I understand that at times, all of this information and methods may in fact sound too good to be true.

Your whole life you hear, 'Life is hard.'

It is programmed into your mind from the time that you were little, so it is no surprise that when trying to find answers about ourselves or the universe, that we would find the solutions to these 'hard' life lessons to be just as challenging.

Thankfully, that is not the case. Life is beautiful. Life is rewarding. Life is easy.

These are the new types of thoughts I would encourage you to start applying to your daily routine. The results and information provided with this shift is nearly instant.

You will be able to see 'clearer' about yourself and others when this shift occurs. It will answer and guide you with all the chaos going on inside of your mind.

Remember, this takes time. Do not become discouraged. You already came this far and you are making vast improvements.

I am proud of you. You are an amazing student.'

It does not take long for silence to again blanket the area.

I release a loud gulp of air from my nose, turning my focus onto the Captain, 'Why do you tell her you are proud of her so much? I think she heard you the first time you said it.'

A soft smile glides against the right side of her mouth, *'Why do you not praise them more? They are doing an amazing job in your game as well as my class. If you want them to be better for you, then you have to be better for them.*

That means appreciating and supporting them. Cutting someone down or belittling them is not helpful to either side. I hope that you have been able to get something from these teachings. I see so much good in you. I just wish you could experience it as well.'

I feel an immediate shift in my energy, 'Ha, okay. Yes, excuse me for not realizing on my own that kidnapping six people and torturing them makes me a 'good' soul.'

The Captain's smile does not waiver at the pain entangled in my words, 'Everyone does things they are not proud of. I am sure you made this decision based off of what you were taught, not who you are. There is a difference.'

I feel the weight of my head tip to the right, 'What do you mean?'

She releases a loud gust of air from her parted lips, 'Did anyone give you a choice to be a game leader or not?'

I feel myself scanning through the files of my mind looking for an answer, 'No. I do not think it is an option. If it is, no one asked me what I thought or felt about it.'

The Captain allows a gentle cascade of laughter to wash over her words, 'Then forgive yourself for your past mistakes and never make them again.
How can you be disappointed in yourself for making a decision with zero or only half of the knowledge? You cannot.
You can only consider it a mistake if you truly did not know any different.
I have been watching you, Arlenm. You have a good heart, do not be so hard on yourself.'

The entire time the information is being downloaded into my brain, I can feel anger bubbling up inside of me at the things she says, 'That is enough!'

It does not take long for my thoughts to echo back to me, silencing the area in its wake.

The Captain inhales a smooth drag of air, 'It is okay. We can talk about it later. I understand.'

A heavy mass of guilt begins to form inside of my chest, 'How are you able to remain so calm, even in the midst of my irrational behavior?'

She nods her head once in my direction, 'I want you to grow. If I take that energy you are giving off and allow it to affect me, nothing will be solved. You will be upset, I will be upset then we will just spread that vibration to every person we come in contact with until it finally wears off naturally, like a virus. I do not want to make you, other people or myself sick. I want to heal and the only way to do that is by connecting the hurt in a person back to the source which is constructed purely out of love.'

My mind stumbles over itself, 'The source of what?'

Her words become weightless, 'Everything. Everything is structured from love. If I am going to war, that is the only thing I need. Anything else, will only cause more destruction.

This concept might be harsh to fully grasp onto in this moment because you are still in the mindset of pain instead of compassion.'

Before I am given a chance to respond, Emily starts to emit an unstable frequency, 'I do not know what I am doing wrong. I feel almost stupid.'

The Captain tips her head to the left, 'Why are you feeling this way? Can you explain it?'

Emily shrugs her shoulders gently, 'I can try, but no promises that it is going to come across clearly to you. I apologize in advance just in case.

So, throughout my life as I am going over everything, I keep finding that a lot of previous choices I made do not make a whole lot of sense to me. In fact, some of them are just downright ridiculous.

I want to make better choices for myself and others, but I am unable to pin-point any source that caused me to act that way in the first place.

I do not know. I suppose, I am getting a little frustrated with myself. There is a lot wrong with me. Do you have any ideas that might help me better understand what is going on?'

The Captain transmits the information in a smooth wave, 'Yes. I *think you are having a hard time connecting fully with your inner self.*

This is really common, especially for anyone who has ever experienced trauma.

Do not worry yourself too much with this.

When your connection with yourself and your guides becomes stronger, that voice of guidance will become louder.

I had experienced something similar in my life as well.

These thoughts are not there to make you do wrong, they are there to help you learn negative and positive energies and their results when you feel the different sides.

Trust yourself, you are beyond magic. You are the beginning and the end of everything that is and ever will be. You can overcome this, just as you have with everything else.

All you have to do is trust that small flicker of love you hear in the back of your mind.

Your guides will always lead you home. Never feel lost, you have always been on track, even when the ride got extremely intense.

You are safe, you are loved.'

CHAPTER TWENTY-EIGHT:

With the space around us once again quiet, I feel a scratch in my throat.

I follow the guide of this urge to speak to the Captain, 'I think you are right.'

She tilts her head more in my direction, 'Right about what? I apologize for the forgetful side of myself.'

I feel an automatic laugh pull itself over my words, 'I thought over what you were explaining earlier and you are right. I need to be more understanding.'

The Captain nods once in agreement, *'Learning the lesson is easy, applying the treatment can be a little trickier. There may be times that you make a small mistake, do not allow it to hinder your progress. Look at it as fine tuning yourself with more information. There are no setbacks, only upgrades.'*

I swallow roughly, 'I do not see why this is such a difficult task.'

She inhales a deep breath, *'The universe has a series of different tests you are given randomly throughout your life to make sure that you have in fact learned the information and know how to apply in in the chaos of a situation.*

If you do not handle it correctly, you will be given the same lesson and test in a slightly different form until you learn the course.

Each 'class' will get more and more difficult, until you have no choice, but to surrender to the truth.

I just wanted to share this information with you. I wish I would have learned it sooner. If I can prevent even just one person in this universe from struggling the way I had to, it would be worth every single second of the pain I had to endure.'

I feel my head nod slowly in response to her fading voice as the room again falls still.

Our attention is shot towards Austin, who has streams of tears flowing down both sides of his cheeks.

The Captain's voice engulfs the area around us, 'Austin, what is causing you to be so disheartened?'

He attempts to breathe in through his nose, but the buildup of sorrow prevents him, *'I don't know what is going on with me, but I feel so different.*

Almost like a weight has been removed from my chest, I can inhale deeply without the normal restriction of burning discomfort.

All of the sudden, it feels like the things that once seemed to matter so much to me, don't seem so major. Then the things that I used to think didn't deserve a second thought have become my whole world.

I feel like I am living inside of a dream, I'm not complaining. It's just scary because I don't want to wake up and lose it.'

A gentle smile begins to form against her sealed lips, *'A shift in mindset and inner healing is all you needed this entire time. These changes are not only expected, they are necessary for you to achieve full growth.'*

The tears are still unstoppable, falling from his jaw line, *'I can feel the vibration of love and compassion pouring from my inner being towards myself and everything else. I adore this feeling. I have finally found the answer to one of my biggest questions. 'How do you give to others without completely destroying yourself in the process?'*

It is really enjoyable to know my heart is once again open. I feel a freedom that I have longed to experience again since I was a child. To be able to love without fear.'

The Captain cannot erase the smile that is now lingering

against her mouth, *'What other changes have you noticed?'*

Austin inhales a soft gust of air, *'For the first time in this life, I can say that I have inner peace.*

I only have thoughts, feelings and actions of love towards myself and others.

When a situation or problem does arise inside of myself, I am finally able to look at it with a view of peace rather than war.

My mind has found a way to quiet itself down when it is no longer needed.

I do not focus on judging myself or others. I allow things to just be how they are, nothing needs to be locked away in the cage of my judgement and opinions.

I will never allow negative energy to consume me the way I once did.

I am starting to understand and accept the balanced of love I give and receive.

I feel like I now have the ability to be myself, without the mental and emotional separation that we experience in these physical forms, I am free.

I honestly never thought that I would ever be able to say that phrase with authenticity. I am so thankful.

It has taken me over two decades to understand that the judgement I faced for being myself was not a block for me to conform, but rather a wall that I needed to take apart.

I am slowly starting to feel my connection with a higher power getting more intense every moment as I watch the miracles swimming by me every second.

The best part is, I am no longer stuck in a vicious cycle of ever switching emotions. I have found that my resting frequency is very intense, but I have never felt happier.

Trust me, I am nowhere near saying that I am complete. I am just recovering. For the first time, I have entered something that will not destroy me.

Thank you for all of your help so far, I am grateful.'

CHAPTER TWENTY-NINE:

Hearing about all of Austin's improvements gives me hope. I find myself getting lost in the ideal version of myself.

My thoughts are shattered by a small giggle engulfing the area, it is branching out from Emily's lungs.

The Captain approaches her with an alluring vibe, 'Are you having a breakthrough?'

Another rumble of laughter is released from her form, it is a sound that I am beginning to find quite enjoyable, 'Yes. It's funny, but I am starting to see less and less separation between me and others, but not just with people, every life source and it is amazing.

This realization is causing me to feel a mixture of emotions.

Sadness because I sometimes feel small in comparison to the world's pain, yet I know the biggest impact I can make is to be an example, not a lecture.

Anger because I know I can't save them all.

Fear because I am unsure if it will ever get better.

Agony because the blood that has been shed from separation, yet it is all released in the same shade.

Anxiety because I want a solution to be put in motion right this second.

Forgiveness for myself and others, for all of the times I thought I was better or below. For each time I spread judgement to someone else or myself just to try to fill the emptiness inside. For every moment I thought I was displaying power, but looking back now, I only see a coward. I forgive myself for all of the times I acted out, when I should have been looking in. For every lie I told, everything I stole. Every look I gave and dollar I shouldn't have saved. I realize now that the only person I was ever competing against was me, but today I am free. I could never thank you enough for making my dreams and happiness become a reality.'

The Captain nods once gently, *'Allow yourself to be engulfed in these feelings and problems that you are and will face. You will then in return find the part in the situation that you are capable of doing. Once you find it, release the rest. Trust the process and allow nothing to shift your thoughts away from the highest vibration you can imagine. You deserve this. Keep your energy elevated by being creative and child-like.'*

CHAPTER THIRTY:

The Captain clears her throat, hoping to draw their attention against her, *'Can you both hear me?'*

Her question is answered by the in-sync movement of their heads nodding in agreement.

A small smile runs against her lips, *'Great. Now, that all of your energy points are clear, open and balanced. I would like to talk to you about a few things before I send you on the rest of your journey alone.*

The first thing I would like to address is your spiritual abilities.

I am unsure if you have any, yet. Now that we have you heading towards the right place for yourselves, you are going to want to help others.

If you do have these abilities, learn everything about your tool. So, when it comes times to use it, you will know exactly what to do.

These abilities can appear at any moment from this point on.'

Emily re-positions her weight between her hips trying to get comfortable, *'What kind of abilities could we have?'*

A gentle laugh runs up the back of the Captain's throat, 'There are many. It is important for your own peace that we just allow whatever is going to come up, to do so naturally. If an ability does appear, your guides will explain how to use them at that time.'

Austin nods his head once in understanding, *'When will we be able to meet our guides?'*

The Captain does not allow much time to pass from his voice leaving our minds, to hers entering, *'They will show up in the same manner as the abilities, one day they will just appear. Like magic.'*

A brief moment of silence drapes heavily over the room.

It is broken by the Captain clearing her throat, "Okay, guys. If you both want to start slowly coming back to where we are on the physical plane. That would be great."

The Captain and I watch as their eyes start to slowly flutter.

Their vision becomes lined with smeared shades from the Captain's form.

She greets them with a kind smile, "How are you guys feeling?"

Austin pulls his shoulders back attempting to relieve some of the tension that resides in his shoulders, "I feel better than when I walked in. I guess, I am not seeing any major changes, but it might be because the information is still trying to fully sink in."

Emily nods in agreement with his description of their current mental and emotional state.

A deep exhale is released slowly from the Captain's lungs, "The things that you are experiencing are completely normal. What you just went through was seven weeks worth of work and years of information all crammed together in the short time that we have shared. Pushing this process is not recommended normally, but due to the uniqueness of your lives and your current position, I felt it was the best thing for all people involved.

You should start to see the results getting stronger when you are able to apply the information in real life situations."

Austin allows her words to fully fade from the air before

his are released, "What if we never use the information?"

The Captain takes a moment to process the question, "When you seek the truth, the universe will use you as an example to not only aid yourself, but others. The guidance will be used in some form or another, the how is not your concern. Just know, when the time is right, that card will be played."

Austin pushes his head forward in a bowing gesture to say a silent, *'thank you'* to the Captain.

It does not take long for another fog of silence to creep over the room.

The mute bubble is broken by the Captain, "That is all the information that I have to share with you at this point. It has been an honor to work with both of you. I know that you will do amazing things from here on out, for yourself and many others.

Thank you for allowing me to guide you this far, but it would appear that I have done my part and now the rest is up to you. I wish you luck on your future journey."

Austin and Emily, both drag themselves to their feet, pushing the upper-half of their form forward.

They speak in coordination with one another, "Thank you."

Austin flashes the Captain a joyous smile while leading Emily out of the small room and back out onto the deck in search of Luke.

I turn in a quick motion, not wanting to miss a single moment of their growth.

Before I make it too far, the Captain's voice stops me, "Arlenm, can I talk to you a minute before you go?"

Irritation overtakes my form as a gasp of air is stolen from my lungs, "Yes?"

She moves at a slow crawl, closing the space between our forms, "One of the hardest things to do is see your own worth. I see it in you and so does Emily and Austin."

An uncontrollable, sarcastic laugh floods my words, "Right. I am sure they see great things in me."

The Captain tries to hold back a sincere laugh, "If they did not care about you, they would have spent the whole time looking for the portal, not trying to save you. If you would just open your eyes, you would begin to see your worth, too."

Before I am able to spew a line of anger, she wraps my form tightly into a hug, hindering me speechless.

CHAPTER THIRTY-ONE:

I quickly pull away from the affection by allowing myself to transition into a mist. I know I cannot let her see that something in her is making me vulnerable.

My form drifts through the air above the ship, where my eyes begin violently scanning the deck in search of my mortals.

It does not take me long to find them. Their forms are progressing at a fair pace as their soles smack against the shallow puddles collecting along the surface of the wood.

They appear to be having a conversation, let's get closer.

Austin turns his attention towards Emily, "I do not get it."

The slight hint of irritation running across his tone grasps at her interest, "You do not get what? Why are you upset?"

Austin shakes his head slightly, "I am not upset. I am confused. We were supposed to have gone through that to help us find Luke, but I did not get any closer to finding him than when I walked through the door. Did you find him?"

Emily's confidence starts to drain from her face, she tilts her head down, "No. I do not know what is going on. The answers will come, we just have to be open to receiving them. Right now, while we are waiting, we can get off of the boat and start searching the world. The rest will work itself out later."

Austin nods gently in agreement, tossing his attention towards the outside of the ship at the roaring water falling from the sky all around them.

His voice breaks through the atmosphere, "Where should we enter at?"

Emily restrains the fear that is trying to leak out against her tone, "I do not think it really matters at this point. He got off the boat a while back. Either way, we have an adventure ahead of us."

She does not even allow a full moment to tick past before she speaks again, "Come on, here."

He is not given enough time to even try to fully process the information of the last five minutes. She uses her body as a barrier to knock his momentum to the left, forcing him to change direction towards the wooden railing.

They move in-sync with one another in every stride. It takes them no times at all to hoist their weight atop the beam. No words are shed between them as they push their bodies forward, sending themselves headfirst into the core of this unknown world.

I allow myself to pass through the curtain of water as well.

The first thing my vision falls against is my mortals connecting with the soft, damp blades of bright pink grass scattered along the soil of this planet.

Loud groans slip out of their throats as their figures come to a rolling stop in the empty meadow. They have now found themselves being the only ones to reside on this stretch of land.

Austin quickly pulls himself to his feet, scoping out the surroundings. Once he confirms that they are currently safe, he stumbles towards Emily, who is attempting to fully extend her limbs as well.

Austin's voice merges with some light chirping coming from behind him in the trees, "Are you okay?"

She cannot help but to release a small laugh, "I am fine. That was really fun. I kind of want to do it again."

Her smile starts to quickly fade as she tips her head to the right. She extends her right hand out to gently stroke the surface of his right shirt sleeve.

She squints her eyes sharply in concern, "Huh, that is really odd. Your clothes are not even damp."

Austin gulps roughly, hoping to control his still rapid breathing, "Yeah, neither are yours."

Emily's eyes sparkle under this information, "I really like this world so far. I have this deep feeling that many amazing things are going to come out of this situation."

Austin nods softly in agreement. He has many thoughts rustling around inside of his mind as a reply, but the center point of his focus is stuck on the surroundings.

The reflective surface of his eyes reveals long blades of wild foliage swaying peacefully from side to side. The slight breeze kisses the spots of his flesh that are bare, sending a sea of goosebumps to wash over him. He inhales a deep breath. The oxygen expands his chest causing a relaxing energy to hold him. The taste of fresh rain bounces around the confines of his mouth as he inhales.

Many trees are randomly scattered throughout the space. Each one wears a jacket of white bark. Thousands of silky, sky blue petals cover the ends of the branches.

The structure allows the orange skyline to blanket the horizon like a backdrop hanging between the twigs.

Emily throws his concentration off by lightly pushing the tips of her fingers into his upper back, "Tag! You are it!"

Austin feels his head snap forward, bringing his mind back to reality.

His vision collides against the back of Emily, who is skipping through the field, a bit ahead of him.

A gentle smirk pulls against the left side of his mouth as he takes off after her.

It does not take them long to notice that the ends of the grass blades are transforming before their eyes.

The tops are shredding themselves into thin slices, not allowing the rips to extend any further than an inch.

Multiple shades of pollen begin clumping together along the loose strands.

The plant life sparks his memory back to Earth. Within a timespan of less than five seconds, he plays through many different points in his past, where he was in a situation that urged him to free himself from the chains of other people's opinions of him, but he always fell short of his own.

Now he finds himself in a similar pattern as the past with the ability to see the obstacle in a different light.

Even with the vast knowledge he now holds, this decision is leaving his mind in a state of uncertainty.

He whispers to himself, '*I really want to have fun in the field, but that is so out of my normal behavior. Well, the behavior that I have allowed Emily to see of me, that is. I fear that if I show this change, our relationship will change.*'

Before the ramble of anxiety has a chance to fully stop echoing through his mind, he attempts to restart this process by taking a deep inhale, '*No. Austin, stop thinking that way. You are not that person anymore. If she truly loves you, she will accept you. If not, then you know how she really feels regarding you. Either way, it is a win. Just relax, calm your mind. You cannot see anything clearly when everything in your brain is in shambles.*'

With his mind now starting to calm down, he begins processing his options.

He hears a soft whisper interrupt his train of thought, '*You know what will make you happy and raise your vibration as well as your friends. There is no reason it is taking you this long to make a choice. Stop doubting yourself. Do it. You do not know how much time you have left in the meadow, make the most of it.*'

Austin breaks his attention off of his inner world and back onto the outer reality.

A small grin glides against the right side of his mouth. He extends his right hand down, grabbing up a handful of grass blades.

His speed intensifies, propelling him to catch up to Emily. Now, no more than two-inches separate their physical forms. He pushes his right arm out towards the side of her face, brushing the pollen in a vertical sweep against her cheek.

The cool sensation of the powder causes her to stop suddenly.

Austin stumbles over his feet attempting to avoid running into her as he cannot control his laughter that is growing by the second from her shocked facial expression that is still smeared against her mouth.

Emily gently glides her fingertips against her jaw.

She carefully examines the shade of white, blue and yellow embedded into her grooved prints, "Wow, this is a side of you I thought only existed in theory."

He tilts his head to the left, "What do you mean?"

She smiles as she wipes the substance onto her shorts, "Raven used to always talk about how annoying you were when you would get into what she would call a '*manic*' episode. All she would share is that you would be really happy and playful when it was just the two of you. I always wondered why you never let us see that part of you."

Austin places his vision towards the ground as he tries to think of a way to respond to how she is reacting to his change.

She does not allow any more time to pass them by before jumping into action. She bends down to gather a bundle of blades herself, smearing the hues against his hair, skin and clothes in an unorganized frenzy of friendly battle.

Laughter erupts into the skyline as Austin and Emily, turn their backs towards one another to gather more ammo for the last leg of the war.

I tilt my angle of vision to the right allowing me to see both of them from the side.

A cool wind brushes over the foliage.

I watch as two people rise out from the grassy carpet in front of them.

Austin feels the heat of bright green eyes staring at him. He tips his head up slowly to see that a beautiful woman is standing before him. A light shade of tan covers her curves, the surrounding pieces of foliage have mended together to form a covering for her chest and hips. Messy strands of her deep brown hair are attempting to become tamed by a flower headband with a strap crafted from vines.

She tilts her head to the right, admiring the blade of grass she is currently twirling between her two, dominate fingers.

Her shoulders push forward, guiding her sturdy hand to run the foliage against his face.

A slight giggle escapes her lips, "I thought I would never find someone like you."

Austin scans her quickly, feeling a light sensation of heat brush against his face, "You were looking for me?"

She nods once in a strong confirmation, no doubt lines her eyes, "You are everything that I have ever wanted in a person on the outside. I have never been so attracted to someone like I am towards you."

I want nothing more in this moment than to stay and eavesdrop on his conversation, but my focus is being yanked towards Emily, who finds herself staring at the bare, sun beaten flesh of an unknown male.

Her vision gives her mind a moment to process what is happening.

The man appears to be a few years older than her. Short, neat, blond hair rests three-inches off of his head. His alluring, gray eyes are locked against her in a captivated gaze.

Out of the bottom of her eyes, she can see the pink slices of grass hanging along his hips in a draping manner that extends to just past the top of his knees.

A loud fit of laughter coming from my left captures my interest. Its source is the woman with Austin.

She speaks to him in a soft glow, "I have so many things that you want."

A pause forms between them as she leans in, resting her lips against his right ear, "Things that you need."

She pulls herself free from his cautious hold, twirling around on the tips of her toes in the fresh carpet.

He watches her every move trying to figure out what her intentions for him truly are.

Without warning, an energetic wave washes over him as a voice creeps into the back of his brain, *'If you agree to be with her solely for a physical connection, you know that the only thing you will be accomplishing is harming yourself and her. To want to be around her, take up her time, use her emotions just for a quick high or a sense of power. That is not love, that is lust and you both deserve more than that.'*

Austin clears his throat allowing thoughts to drain from his parted lips, "I am sorry. You are a beautiful woman, but do not let that be the thing you put on your hook when trying to catch somebody to love. Someone who deeply cares for you will think you are the most amazing woman in the world, not because of your hair, your makeup or your body.

They will think that what is going through your mind is

art. Your eyes will be the purest form of relief they can find because it is the window to heaven that they can only find within you. Your smile is going to be contagious and your laugh will leave him breathless. They will care about you for who you are, the rest of the stuff, it will not last anyway. You deserve to be someone's investment, not their pass time."

She tries to conceal her smile as she whispers, "You deserve that, too."

Austin swallows the emotion building up in the back of his throat, "Do not worry, someone great is going to find you. Keep your energy at a high level, so that he can spot you, even in the middle of all the chaos."

Without giving her much time to construct a reply, he flashes her a fast smile and takes off in the direction of Emily.

I allow my senses to zoom in on my last remaining, female pawn.

She has her right-hand laying against his left, upper arm, "I apologize. My attention, love and time is already being held by the most wonderful man in the entire universe. I am blessed to have him. Actually, I am on my way to meet him right now. I hope you can understand, it is not because what you are offering is not good enough. It is because I already found what I was looking for. Why would I keep searching when what I have is more than just a physical offering, it is an internal contract?"

Before Emily has a chance to step out of the conversation fully, Austin locks his arm around hers, pulling her form into a stumbling manner away from the two creatures.

Emily releases a harsh gasp as her body drags onwards. She tosses her attention over her left shoulder.

Her pupils expand as she records the moment that the man and woman share their first look.

Without a verbal word spoken between the two, they take off running full speed towards one another.

When they reach roughly three-feet away from each other, they both jump into the air.

The moment their toes leave the sturdy foundation of the ground, their physical forms are stripped away from their cores. It reveals two, misty, beautiful and pure creations that combine in the wind. They cling to each other as if the small fragments of air that has collected between them is too much space for them to bear apart.

Emily's bottom lip drapes down gently, "Whoa. Austin, did you see that?"

Austin nods quickly, still trying to calm his pounding heart, "The physical aspect of love leaves us empty. Only to be touched by one's soul will allow you to feel whole."

CHAPTER THIRTY-TWO:

Austin is in the lead now. His right arm is twisted in an uncomfortable position behind his back, hanging onto Emily's fingers loosely.

Emily's vision is mostly covered by the puddle of sweat leaking through the back of Austin's shirt.

She steps on a loose rock, shooting her body to the left giving her a clear flash of what lays just beyond Austin's form.

Her pupils widen, "What are they doing?"

Austin speaks with a rough tone, "Who?"

Emily releases her hand from Austin's grip. He stops walking, hoping to find a reason to her behavior.

She extends her right, index finger across her chest.

Austin casually turns around to see three figures seated around a table, placed off to the side, in the middle of absolutely nothing.

The sound of a male voice glides against my pawns' ears as nothing more than a mass of jumbled nonsense.

A young man sitting at the table catches a glimpse of the humans.

He uses his right hand to offer a friendly gesture towards them.

Austin immediately starts to advance in their direction.

Emily stumbles over her feet trying to keep up, "Wait. Something about this feels off, or is it just me?"

Austin shrugs his shoulders, "I am unsure at the moment. All I know, is that the Captain said fear is the only thing standing between us and everything we ever wanted. Right now, fear is trying to prevent me from finding Luke. I think we should take the risk."

Emily quickly scans the surroundings, hoping something will pop up that is more promising than the circular, wooden table that lays on top of roughly four-feet of the pink carpet.

Unfortunately, she does not receive the mirage she so desperately craved.

All of the occupants are male in the physical sense of gender. They appear to be under two and a half decades old.

They are all identical, not a single detail can be found that separates the clones.

Emily scans their figures one more time, just in case she missed something from the first two times.

She starts with their hair. It has a soft curl, adding just a touch of volume to the light brown strands. Each piece of their groomed follicles are swept to the left, sprouting no more than two-inches from their scalp.

Their strong jawline and cheekbones are tightly wrapped in a bottled shine of bronze. All three are covered in a polyester, three-piece, teal suit with a plain, white button down with only five of the loops fastened.

Austin and Emily refrain from getting any closer to the table.

The man, who waved to them earlier allows his hazel eyes to meet theirs in an intense glare.

A smile tries to slide against the left side of his face, "Welcome. Please, have a seat."

Austin nods twice, proceeding to advance in a confident stride.

Emily follows closely behind, trapped in a bubble of unexplained anxiety.

She attempts to relax her mind by whispering to herself, "Everything is okay, you are safe. Remember, nothing occurs without reason."

Her voice becomes drowned out by the man directly across from them, "I am sorry, but I thought there was three of you."

Austin allows his weight to fold into an empty chair.

Emily tails his movements, the seat cracks under her weight as she plops herself down roughly in the one on his right.

Austin drapes his left arm casually over the backrest of the empty sitting placement beside him.

The tips of his fingers tap a gentle, unknown melody against one of the pin wheels, "We are just as shocked as you. We do not know where he is. We were given the information that a creature in your world has him. He goes by the name of Dalton. Do you know where we might be able to find him?"

The young man to the left of the pawns clears his throat by releasing a small laugh, "Dalton does not have your friend."

Austin leans the weight of his head to the right, "How are you so sure?"

The clone on the right, re-positions his hips, "Dalton would not hurt or kidnap anyone. He is the nicest guy we have ever met, without a doubt. Trust us, you have the wrong guy."

This information sparks Austin's interest, "Okay, so if Dalton does not have my friend, then who do you think does?"

Before any of the men have a chance to respond to his question, three women appear out of thin air. Each one is positioned to the right of one of the clones.

They are also identical to one another. Their skin is flawless and pale. Their lips are bright red and full.

The blue tints of their vision remind my mortals of ice.

A chill runs down Emily's back, she throws her gaze towards the grass causing a blur of their blonde, wavy locks to smear against her vision.

The woman across the table leans forward slightly, snapping the fingers of her dominate hand.

The sound of her gesture echoes through the empty hands of nature as plates of food appear upon the flesh of wood.

Austin cannot restrain a glow of amazement as he looks down at the rolled cabbage on each of their plates.

Emily straightens her posture, scanning the men, waiting for a sign that it is safe to indulge on the food.

The man across the table, places his right elbow against the top of the dining furniture. He takes a casual bite out of the item. His eyebrows rise in response to his delight.

Austin glances in Emily's direction, nodding once, implying to her that the meal is in fact safe. They devour every last crumble in a matter of seconds.

Austin enjoyed it so much, he even licks the remaining flavors from his fingers.

The man to the left of Austin, tilts his head to the side, "Those went down easy. I am surprised that you did not pace yourselves more. Tell me, have you ever been on this before or is it your first time?"

Emily tries to conceal a nervous laugh, "No. We have never had them, they are good though. What is in it?"

A cloud of uncertain silence casts over the table.

The three men share looks of amusement between each other.

The man across the way rubs his hands clean over the half-eaten roll left on his plate.

He uses the tips of the first, three fingers of his left hand to slide the dish forward, "It is constructed form different plants found in the local meadows. All of the ingredients combined will show effects of hallucinogens. The first symptoms should start to appear any second now. They can last up to four hours of Earth time."

Emily can feel beads of condensation building against her palms.

She violently rubs her flesh against her thighs, leaning into Austin, "I am scared."

Austin can feel a string of fear trying to crawl up the back of his throat, "It is okay. I am here, it will not last forever. We will be okay. Just try to stay calm and relaxed."

Emily inhales slowly, pushing her weight back into a lounging position, *'It is okay. You are okay. There is nothing you can do to change it now. Just ride it out, like Austin said, it will not last forever.'*

The man on their right, leans forward slightly in Austin's direction, "Is she okay?"

Austin side glances at Emily, extending his right arm out, underneath the table to grab hers.

His voice stays calm and confident, "Yes. She is fine. Thank you. So, what happens now?"

The man shrugs, a sly grin forms against his lips, "Whatever you want, buddy. That is completely up to you."

Austin turns his head towards Emily, his bottom lip hangs open. He is hoping words of comfort are released to sooth her anxiety, but only mumbles escape.

He turns his attention back onto the rest of the table, hoping that one of these men will have a better way with their words than him.

His pupils dilate in shock when he realizes that there is nothing left of any of them besides empty chairs, messy plates and the mark on their memory.

Austin shifts his focus against Emily, knowing the reality of what just happened is going to trigger something negative in her at any moment.

Emily can feel the quickened pound of her heart thumping against the confines of her ribs.

Austin stands in a smooth motion. He extends his right hand down towards her. She quickly fills the empty space with her damp, cool flesh.

He leads her away from the table in a hopeful vibration towards the direction they last saw Luke.

Once they reach twenty-feet from the dining area, Austin digs his toes into the ground preventing them from advancing any further. He does not think it is an intelligent move to wander into the unknown world in their current state.

Austin releases her hand, lowering his form towards the ground in a laying position. Emily quickly follows suit.

The energy flowing through her is so intense, she fears that she may be sick.

She feels herself become more restless with every passing second. She shoots her body into an upright, sitting placement trying to regain control over her rapid breath.

Austin mimics her gestures, placing his left arm in a draping manner over her shoulders.

He allows words to dance off of his tongue in a soothing manner, "Everything is going to be just fine. It is just the high affecting you. Take a few, deep breaths and lay back down. Completely relax every inch of your body, try putting yourself into a state of inner peace. Remember what the Captain said, why worry when there are only two outcomes for every situation and one truth."

Emily tries to distract her current disobedient mind, "What are the two outcomes, again?"

Austin tilts his focus down towards the swaying blades, "You either make it or you don't."

Emily smiles to herself as a small drop of emotion trails down her cheek, "And, the truth?"

Austin speaks in a crackling tone, "Either way, it was meant to be."

CHAPTER THIRTY-THREE:

Time passes by me slow as they have regained a hold of themselves enough to be able to ride out the trip that put Emily on the verge of a stroke.

Emily begins to show signs of old, mental patterns that are creeping through her mind. I allow myself the freedom to connect with the activity.

Emily flutters her eyes open slightly, with the deep feeling that someone else is now occupying the space as well.

The warm rays of the sun sting her vision as a shadow begins to lift off of the figure, revealing it to be Morgan.

Emily does not even fully allow the information to sink in before pulling herself to her feet in excitement of a familiar face.

Morgan fills the empty air, "I did not want to scare you. I was just going to wait until you woke up to make my presence be known, but now you are awake, so it is all good again."

Emily feels rounds of unstable thoughts beginning to be fired in every direction inside of her head, "What are you doing here? I cannot believe this! I am so glad you are okay. I thought that I was never going to be able to see you again."

She rushes towards Morgan, embracing her in a tight hold.

Morgan pulls her head back slightly, "I am fine. It is you that I am worried about."

Emily tips her chin up slightly in confusion, "What do you mean?

Why are you worried about me?"

Morgan's eyes melt over her with sympathy, "I know how you can get when things are progressing without a plan. Not to even mention, how frightened you must be feeling from the food. Then on top of it all, the best thing you have for comfort is Austin. Which is not saying much."

Emily attempts to cover up a sarcastic laugh with a growing smile, "Morgan, I really appreciate that these events made you think of me, it means a lot. However, I am not the same person anymore. I had a rocky start when everything first happened, but then Austin helped a lot. We have both changed so much, it is going to be a new adjustment for anyone who knew us before this."

Morgan quickly places her arms in a crossed gesture along her chest, "You are right, you did change, but for the worst. People do not change for the better, Emily."

Emily can feel a sting of pain forming behind her eyes, "They do, but only when they are given the room."

Emily sits up sharply trying to control her breathing.

The brush of the cool air feels soothing against her flesh. She turns her attention towards Austin, relief washes over her when she realizes what she had just experienced was only in her mind.

She gently rolls her fingers against Austin's left arm, hoping to wake him. Only, he is too far inside of his own episode to come out into reality just yet.

Come on, we must know what is unfolding without us.

Tapping into Austin's mind gets easier every time. I slowly scan the area until my vision bumps against two figures.

146

Austin and Raven appear to be engulfed in a heated string of words.

Raven's voice cracks against the stale air, "What do you mean you are not going to give me another chance?"

Austin flashes her a fast grin, "I apologize. It is not personal. We were just not meant to be together forever. I look back now and laugh to myself when I think about all the times that I thought we were. I have found peace and I hope you can, too."

Austin turns to his left, scanning the area looking for Emily to help guide him in the right direction.

The silence in the air is shattered by Raven's desperation, "What about your fear of being alone? You cannot stand to be alone, you even told me on countless occasions that you would rather die than have to face a single day of this life alone. Which can only mean that you found someone else. Who is she? Do I know her? It is one of the Goddess from world two, isn't it? You started acting so strange after that level. Why didn't you just stay behind in that world then if they were so important to you? Speaking of things that are of value. Why haven't you come back to save me, yet?"

Austin can feel a light tug of a smile trying to break against his mouth.

Her eyes widen in shock as her voice grows colder, "What is so funny? Nothing about this is funny. Why are you laughing?"

Austin attempts to control his tone, but the humor still surrounds each letter, "It is not that I think the situation is funny. I am just so happy. I cannot stop smiling."

Another burst of chuckles is released from his throat.

She uses this time to vocalize her emotions, "Because you are getting to see me?"

He shakes his head in response, "No. Because I am so thankful that I am no longer who I was when I met you. I never thought I would live to see that day that I would be able to say what is going through my head right now with complete honesty, but it has finally arrived."

Austin wraps her in a fast embrace before releasing her just as quickly.

Raven tilts her head, lost in thoughts of confusion, "Say what? What is going on?"

Austin can feel the warmth of bliss flowing from his chest, "Raven, thank you for not loving me. You taught me how to love myself enough to know that I am complete by myself. Thank you, for making me realize what I truly deserve. Even when I could not see it myself."

Austin awakens in a fast motion.

He squints his left eye giving himself the ability to try and grasp his barring with his right.

He scans the area right to left, halfway through the rotation he notices that peeking at him from inside of the blades are shield shaped, glowing, blue eyes.

The one to the left closes sharply, giving me a quick wink of acknowledgement.

Austin stops looking around, closing his eyes sharply just to re-open them a minute later to see that the eyes have vanished.

His flowing thoughts are interrupted by Emily lightly laying her arm on his left shoulder, "Hey. Are you okay?"

Austin nods his head slowly, a growing grin slides against his mouth out of her view, "Yeah, I am great. I feel a lot better after calming down. I think it is still in our system a little bit, but nothing we cannot manage. How are you feeling? Did you get to meditate? I tried to make sure you were relaxed before settling myself in."

Emily bobs her head in rhythm with his vocal expression that is still echoing through her mind, "I am better. I have never seen you so caring and understanding as I have here lately."

Austin inhales a deep breath of satisfaction, "Yes, I know. I have neglected my true self for far too long. I am enjoying the freedom."

Austin pulls himself into a wobbly stance and starts walking forward, hoping to lead them towards the next adventure.

Emily rushes her feet to try and catch up, "Austin, wait. Are you sure that you are okay?"

Austin tips his head back in a playful sway coming to a stop, "Emily, I have never been happier in my entire life."

Emily sends him a fast, fake smile, "So, the past is still not bothering you? Not even a little bit?"

Austin does not allow her doubt to consume him, "I am not saying it will not ever try to test me again. All I am saying is that if it does, I will get through it. I signed a contract for my soul, I am not going anywhere until it is my time. So, I am just going to sit back and enjoy the ride."

Emily trips over her tongue nervously, "I fear I might be doing something wrong with my transitioning. I am not where you are at, not even close. I might have fought the physical obstacles of my pain, but the mental and emotional cycles are still destroying me every time I think I am getting ahead."

Austin inhales slowly giving her emotions a chance to decrease in intensity before he speaks, "You already know the answer. You just said it. The only thing you have to do now is overcome the scenarios in yourself one, last time and you will be freed from the lesson. You are so close, do not give up on yourself now. Life will either walk beside you or drag you. Always do your best to keep up."

Emily feels a mixture of emotions colliding in her chest. She runs into his figure with such agony, it nearly knocks him over.

Loose tears fall against the surface of his shirt as he whispers, "Bliss is up the road, but we will never find it staying still. Come on."

CHAPTER THIRTY-FOUR:

Austin keeps a firm hold on Emily's right hand as they advance through the meadow at a fairly fast pace.

Austin stops progressing sharply causing Emily to run into the back of him. A loud gust of air is ripped from her lungs upon impact.

She rushes her mouth to release a whisper, "Why are we stopping?"

Austin's tone remains calm, "There is a woman sitting in the middle of the field. We should go see if she is alright."

Emily leans all of her weight against her right leg, hoping to get a better reading on this woman.

Upon first glance, Emily becomes flooded with negative emotions, "I do not think we should stop. I am sure there is another way around. The last thing you want to do is add more trouble to your life. You just got rid of all that crap you had. Why bring in more?"

Austin spins around to face her, his eyes are sparkling in a way that she has never seen before, "Emily, I have waited my entire life to finally be able to have enough courage to be myself. I want to do this."

Emily huffs violently, "Why do you have this deep desire to save everyone?"

Austin swallows roughly trying to ensure his own feelings before sharing them with her, "Because all I ever wanted was someone to be brave enough to meet me from their own perspective, not the rest of the worlds."

Emily shakes her head slowly, "But, you can see the truth now. You can read energy. You have the ability to prevent yourself from never getting hurt again. Why would you not use this power as a shield?"

Austin releases a small laugh, "Emily, energy might never lie and maybe, right now I am not getting the best reading, but if someone else is in distress and I do not stop, it will haunt me for the rest of my life. I am not saying to be naïve. What I am saying, is you have to make sure you listen to what you are hearing. Not what someone else is saying, not what your fear is saying, but what you are saying. Because of the Captain, I can finally trust myself enough to know I will stay, walk or run when the time to act is needed."

Emily extends her left hand out to clamp around his right forearm, "Austin, I think this is one of the tests that the Captain was telling us about."

Austin's eyes shine as his smile grows deeper, "I know and I am going to pass it. Trust me."

Emily is starting to realize that she has entered a never-ending battle. Her head nods slightly in approval following him for every advancement.

Austin sits down in the grass in front of the unknown woman. Her structure is slim and boney. She extends only five-feet from the world's surface. A light shade of cream runs against her flesh, making her green eyes ten times warmer. Tight, burgundy curls surround her strong facial structure.

The woman peeks up slightly to investigate the approach of my humans.

Austin tilts his head to the side, "Are you from Earth?"

She does not greet him with eye contact, "No, I am from here. I live in the city. I got really mad at my boyfriend for taking too long when he said he was going to go get *'food'*. How does it take someone over two-hundred and forty minutes to get something to eat? That is just the beginning. We would have to sit here for a very long time if I were to share the entire story with you."

Austin grins playfully, "That is not necessary. There is nothing you can do to fix what was. Thank you for the offer. However, I can assist with the issue that made you run away into the forest. I—"

His voice is shattered by the woman's tone, "I swam."

Austin's brow pushes inward slightly, "Can you explain what you mean?"

A touch of irritation lines her tone, "You said that I ran into the forest. I did not run, I swam."

Austin nods once in confirmation, "Of course. My apologizes. I can help, so you do not go swimming off into the unknown every time something happens that makes you uncomfortable. Now, when you—"

The static crack of her voice coming alive echoes through the trees, "I have to be right, all of the time. You were wrong, so I had to correct you."

Austin releases a soulful chuckle, "I understand it can be difficult to live in such circumstances where you know everything. Since you are always right, I will leave you to discuss this matter further with yourself. I wish you the best of luck on your travels."

It does not take them long to pick up a good pace towards the west.

Austin allows his thoughts to flow freely, "So, I was thinking when we find Luke. Maybe, we can get him to go with us back onto the boat, so the Captain can put him through that class, too."

Emily's eyes widen sharply, "We need to hold off on that thought until we see him. We do not know what us going down this journey affected outside of us. You heard the Captain. This awakening will cause everyone in our soul family to grow as well. Right now, I have other questions racing through my mind. How do you do that?"

Austin shrugs in an unknowing sway, "Do what?"

Emily exhales loudly through her nose, "How do you just leave a situation like that? No mess, no regrets, not even a single acknowledgement of it ever happening. Not to mention, staying out of old patterns. I do not know what is scaring me more, your growth or my lack of."

Austin places his hands in a comforting manner on her shoulders, "You know all of this information. You have the answers. There is no difference between me and you. The only thing you have to do is completely release everything you know and from this moment on, when something no longer serves you, walk away and never look back. Leave the baggage by the front door and carry on. If it is not currently affecting you, then why would you allow it to continue to hurt you?"

Emily brushes off his affection, leading the way closer to Luke, "Well, what if she comes back? Are you not worried about that?"

Austin's head shakes slowly, "Then I will deal with it then. Right now, I am free."

She inhales a deep breath as she attempts to gather control of her nerves. Her vision is grazed by the fast blur of the woman swimming in their direction at a fast pace.

Emily rolls her eyes slightly, "Well, you were free."

Before he has a chance to question her disapproval, the other woman's voice explodes through the area, "Wait. Please, help me. I am sorry that I was being difficult earlier. Please, do not leave me out here. I do not know my way home."

Austin nods his head firmly, "When it comes to your relationship, you will never be fully at ease in the arms of someone when you do not feel comfort in the hold of your own. If you love and respect yourself, you will not have to concern yourself with thoughts of what your partner is or is not doing. When you are given a dose of the truth you will be able to stand strong. Your worrying is not hurting him whether he is or is not cheating. The only person being hurt right now is you and the abuser is not him, it is you."

The woman's bottom lip drops slightly, "That is it? That is your big advice? That was not help, that was you being rude."

Austin nods once in her direction, "The truth can sound cruel in two situations. If it is based off of an opinion or if you are not ready to hear it."

Austin does not utter another line of assistance as he turns to walk away.

Emily beams with satisfaction at the situation as she runs to his right side, nearly tripping over her own feet, "I am so proud of you. That was amazing."

Austin shrugs his shoulders in a relaxed manner, "It is how I should have done things."

Emily nods her head slowly, putting all of her attention onto the scenery that is blossoming and exploding with life around them.

A strong gust of air brushes against the empty plot of land. Inside of the currents, are thousands of colorful specs of pollen.

Emily's eyes drain with bliss as she watches the tiny dots form a picture of her and Raven held in a loving embrace.

The image sends her mind spiraling through the details of what their relationship really was, beyond the veil of delusion.

A shot of frustration and pain runs along her chest, "How do you not have anger towards her for what she did to you?"

Austin exhales slowly under the topic, "Who are you referring to?"

Emily can feel tension rise into her temples, "Raven."

Austin smiles, giving himself a moment to sort out his thoughts, "She was just a physical guide for both of us. She is not a bad person, simply a harsher lesson. How can I hate someone, who at one point loved me so much, they signed a contract to come to a physical plane to completely destroy me because she knew that when she did, I would stand up and become ten times stronger than when she knocked me down. I love all of my past guides. I just realize their work is done for now and that is okay. We both are onto greater things."

Emily tilts her head to the right, "How come it is so easy for you to blow off what happened to you?"

Austin's eyes become lost in the vacant, orange hues of the sky, "I never wanted people to feel sorry for me because of what happened to me. I never wanted to find a way to erase what occurred. All I ever wanted was the truth of why we were here, what the rules are, what I am trying to accomplish with my time here, a stronger connection to the Divine and all other questions that were the true source of my pain. Now, that I have found that truth, the rest just does not matter."

Emily squints her eyes tighter, "She abused you for thirteen years. She made every day you were together a complete nightmare and you just are going to forgive her? I do not think she deserves your forgiveness."

Austin begins walking with a joyous stride, "Let me ask you something. Have you ever made a mistake in your life where it caused someone else to be hurt?"

Emily forces a sarcastic laugh, "Yeah, but the mistakes I made were little. I never have and I never would treat someone the way she treated us."

His eyes fall towards the yellow pollen collecting against his worn-out sneakers, "That may be true. When you did those things that hurt someone else, did you mean to do them or was it just an uncontrollable, outburst of pent-up pain that just happened to come out onto them?"

Emily's shoulders drop slightly, "It was just something that happened. I felt really guilty after, but the damage was already done."

Austin nods his head in-sync with her vocal expressions, "And, did you feel this guilt until they forgave you?"

She pushes her head forward in a slow gesture of agreement.

He inhales a short breath of fresh air, "Then we have to forgive her to free us from the pain."

Emily can feel the betrayal running against her tongue, "But, that is too easy. That is, it? Just let her go on with her life and be happy with no repercussions?"

Austin tries to control his vocal speed, "Us forgiving her releases us. It will help her journey as well, but before it can she has to first battle herself. When you hurt someone and they forgave you, the guilt did not go away. It became less heavy, but the pain still crippled you when you were alone. You could not run from it. It was always there until you got the courage to face it."

Emily feels a soft smile break across her mouth as a trail of fears run down her right cheek, "Thank you."

CHAPTER THIRTY-FIVE:

Austin and Emily find themselves stopped at the end of the grass lands, looking into the city.

Right now, the only thing they are able to see is a vacant, paved, city street and large buildings that are constructed from steel beams and glass panels. The changing rays of pink shine against the reflective surface giving them no clues to what might reside inside.

Emily speaks in a positive tone, "Wow, this looks a lot like Earth."

Austin nods in agreement, "All of the words have had characteristics of Earth and humans more than not. People just become so caught up in the differences, they end up blinding themselves from the similarities. Are you ready to take the first steps into the next adventure?"

Emily responds by nudging them onwards. The moment they step an inch onto the asphalt, a jet stream of powerful, rushing bubbles are being pushed in a vertical movement.

It raises their bodies into the air allowing them to hover three-feet from the ground.

Large smiles erupt on both of their faces. Austin begins twirling his body around in the zero-gravity illusion.

He throws all of his weight back, kicking his feet into the air attempting to complete a flip when another stream of bubbles shoves them forward at a fast pace.

They are tossed through the currents in a jumbled fashion, unable to regain their structure.

A fast jerk pushes their forms roughly onwards causing them to slam into an invisible barrier.

Austin uses his right, index finger to guide Emily's attention in an upwards manner, "It is because of the traffic light."

Her pupils widen sharply, seeing that inside of the colors are symbols that represent a swim zone.

She scans the area quickly. Now, that they are out of the alley. The streets are covered with people walking along the sidewalks and paddling through the streets. All of them at first glance appear to mimic the creatures of Earth for every hair.

Emily peers around at all the businesses while whispering to Austin, "We are severely under dressed. Maybe, we can find something to change into."

Austin nods in agreement when his eyes catch against a sign that reads, 'New you? New style.'

A small smirk lifts the left side of his mouth, "Come on, I found one that sounds fitting."

The light taps of water leaking onto the concrete enters their mind as they step out of the street.

Austin pulls the silver handle of the door to the business open allowing a powerful smell of mixing cologne to file out of the doorway.

They waste no time venturing into the space.

A man in a slim fit, three-piece, yellow stained suit greets them, "What can I do for the two of you?"

Before they have a chance to indulge them in conversation, he speaks again.

The movement of his lips cause his dark green eyes to burn brighter, "Did you really have to drag water through here?"

Austin peers down at the beads of condensation before shooting his attention towards the worker, who is now rushing their direction with two towels crumbled in his palm.

Anxiety fuels his every stride, "Here, you can use these to dry off."

Austin finds comfort in the soft fabric of the light hue of pink. He rubs the material in a slow, downwards movement against his face.

He inhales every drop of the fragrance from its last wash.

The worker appears to get anxious from their presence.

He runs the fingers of his right hand through the short strands of his brown hair, "Okay, I think it is time for you to get out before someone sees you. This business cannot take another hit, right now."

Austin squints his eyes, "Why is us being in here bad for the store? We need something more suitable to wear for the environment."

The worker releases a strong laugh of amusement,

"Well, you certainly will not be able to afford anything in here. You might be able to find something that better fits your budget at the store a few blocks over. It caters to your kind."

Emily tosses her head back, "Austin, how badly are we standing out here?"

The worker does not give Austin a chance to respond, "Horribly. I could see you from miles away. You both look like you have been living in the wilderness."

Austin cannot hold down his laughter, "We have."

He then tilts his attention to the right, "Emily, we will find Luke. Do not worry. If he will not help us, someone else will."

The man squints his vision sharply, crossing his arms over his chest, "Wait here. Do not move, I will be right back."

Austin releases a small note of laughter as he and Emily share a look of confusion.

It does not take them long to attempt to distract their minds by gazing around the small show area.

They are currently standing three-feet from the entrance. Directly in front of them is a large, wooden desk that acts as a checkout counter. The light brown flesh brings to life the darker wall panels that encase them. The covering beneath their feet is a tightly woven, flat blanket of cream-colored fabric.

The entire space is littered with suits, dress shoes and accessories.

Before they have a full chance to intake the surroundings, the man is returning into their view with a single sheet of paper in his left hand.

He is moving at such a sharp pace, the edges fold along the structure of his hand as he advances forward.

Every drop of excitement in his form drains from his bottom lip, "Are you Emily Johnson and Austin Parker?"

Austin nods once, "Yes. Why do you ask?"

The man turns the paper around. Their eyes widen slightly, seeing sketched images of their own faces drawn below the bold, black ink that reads, '**MISSING**'.

Their vision grazes against their full names smeared underneath the appropriate picture.

Austin allows a childlike laugh to fall into the air, "That is really cool. Do you know who posted the ad?"

The man skims over the propaganda quickly seeking the source, "Ah, yes. It is right here at the bottom a Mr. Lucas Myers."

Austin and Emily share a strong shot of confusion.

Before they have a chance to speak, the man releases a phrase of letters, "There is no number, but it says any information regarding the missing persons should be mailed or expressed in person at 222 sunset Dr. Suite 444."

Austin nods once in the direction of the worker, "Can you explain to us how to get there?"

A loud exhale of annoyance stales the air, "Yes, but you

cannot go in there dressed like that. Go pick something out to wear from the racks. Please, try to keep the outfit under five-hundred dollars."

Austin shoots the man a fast grin before heading towards the endless options.

The man crosses his arms over his chest allowing his eyes to cut into Emily, "You, too. Go. Hurry, we do not have all day."

Emily's face flushes with excitement as she zooms past Austin on the floor, hurrying into the racks.

She calls back to Austin, "This is the best world, yet! I am so excited! I have not been able to wear a suit for years!"

Hearing this information only causes his smile to grow wider.

It does not take long for them to sort through the many colors and styles that are available before finding one they are comfortable in.

Austin steps out of the dressing room in a full black, two-piece suit while a white, button down hugs his torso. The entire outfit is held together by a solid, black tie. His aching feet finally feel relief now that his black, dress socks are covered by a matching pair of new shoes.

A large grin cannot be wiped from Emily's mouth as she admires the two-piece suit she picked out that is a beautiful cream in color. It is paired with the same dress shirt as Austin with a matching shade of shoes.

Their attention is shot towards the worker, who clasps his hands together at the sight, "You both look wonderful.

One more thing before you head out on your own."

The room remains silent as he walks towards the front desk, gathering an unlabeled, plastic, spray bottle that is dyed black in color.

He speaks in a calming manner, "This will keep the water in the streets from getting you soaked while traveling."

They feel the light spray of liquid coating their forms, the subtle smell of lemon fills their nasal passages.

The worker replaces the lid on the bottle, "So, I do have one favor to ask of you. Since I did the kind gesture for you."

Austin's smile beams, "Of course, anything."

He nods once, replaying the thought again in his mind before releasing it into the air, "When you see Mr. Myers, could you please tell him I gave you the best service possible?"

Emily jumps into the Conversation, "Yes. What is your name?"

The man raises his open, right palm out towards her, shaking his wrist, "No names. Just the title of the store will be fine. Thank you."

CHAPTER THIRTY-SIX:

Austin and Emily decide that they would rather walk than take the jet stream, not wanting to miss the address in this new and exciting environment.

Austin is traveling at a pretty fast pace.

Emily wants to keep up, but her anxiety is bringing her down, "Hey, I have to tell you something really weird that happened to me when I was in the dressing room earlier."

Austin nods once, "What happened?"

Her gaze falls towards the pebbles of rock embedded into the concrete, "I think I saw part of one of my guides."

Austin raises his eyebrows in surprise, "That is amazing. What did you see?"

The air between them becomes stale as she plays the memory back in her mind, hoping to capture every detail, "It was a woman. She was beautiful. She had on a flowing, white robe that was draped loosely against her skin which was glowing. It was so light in color, I thought I would go blind if I continued to stare at her any longer."

Austin's eyes sparkle, "That is astonishing. Did she say anything to you? Did anything else happen?"

Emily shakes her head slightly, "No, that was it. I got a little afraid and then she went away. I have not seen her since."

He can detect the sadness welling up behind her words, "Do not be sad. This is just the beginning. You will see her again. You cannot allow your fear of the new to prevent you from enjoying it."

Emily spills the hope rising in her form, "You think she only left because I got afraid?"

Austin slowly nods, "Yes. She loves you. She does not want you to feel scared or uncomfortable in the same way that you would not want to make me feel that way."

She attempts to allow his words to fully sink in, but he speaks again before she has a chance, "Here. 222 sunset Dr."

Emily raises her eyebrows as she examines the large, glass building that must reach at least twenty stories high.

Austin takes one glance at them in the mirror.

A small smile overtakes his lips as he thinks, *Wow, I have not seen myself this put together in years. To be honest, there was a time when I thought that I would never see it again."*

His mind drifts towards the structure as he guides Emily into the alluring entrance.

Their eyes dart around the area to see a lobby.

The space is completely empty besides them. A short, white carpet lines the floor. A row of contemporary couches are positioned in front of the four, huge panels that look out into the street. Each seating area is separated by a small, wooden end table that has black and white swirls of beautiful brush strokes.

On the far, right wall runs a stream of water across the entire space. A garden of assorted size and color rocks rest at the bottom. Every two-feet, flat spheres of white light can be seen peeking through the space in between the pebbles.

Emily scans the left side of the room. A four-foot-long, solid gray, check-in desk is facing them. A lonely, matching, rolling chair is currently empty, positioned behind the structure.

Austin gently taps Emily's right, upper arm with the tips of his fingers, "Come on, we need to take the elevator."

Austin's stride is overflowing with excitement, the elevator doors open in response to their presence.

Once inside, the steel reflective walls remind them of the same invention of Earth. A line of glowing, light blue lights are numbered one through twenty-two.

Austin's hand knocks against the appropriate button.

A wave of water begins rushing into the structure. It happens at such a fast rate. They are not given a chance to realize what is going on.

The next thing they know, the molecules have them suspended in the air.

Another shove of waves comes shooting up from the bottom, pushing their forms in a fast, vertical movement.

Their figures stop moving sharply as a steel grate is being extended six-feet beneath them.

The whites of their eyes strain as the water level begins to drop.

Once their chests are revealed to the surface, Austin

slams his hands in a downwards push of excitement.

The echo of his flesh colliding with the water's edge rings through the space, "That was absolutely amazing. I cannot wait to go back down!"

Emily drops her gaze towards her smeared reflection now around her waist, "It was not fun. It was irritating and now the doors will not open until all of the water drains and it is taking forever."

Austin does not allow his smile to waiver, "Emily, you have to stop resisting change on a physical and emotional level. Everything will always work itself out, just do not drag your feet.

You have to be like Arlenm. He is able to turn into any form, at any time. No matter what the situation will bring, he does not worry about the future. His confidence, faith and patience are held within his ability to become whatever he needs at the time, we all have this strength.

For example:

When the elevator started filling with water, you should have not allowed your fear to turn the transition into something negative.

You should look at every change no matter how big or small as an exciting, new adventure physically, mentally and spiritually.

Do not worry about the last adventure or the next. The current path you are on right now, at this moment, is the most important. It deserves all of your focus because you do not want to look back with regrets. You only make mistakes when you are rushing something. It is the smallest details that make the largest impacts.

It is okay, everything is good. Do not stress over your mind for no reason."

Emily's voice cracks against the water flooding their

ankles, "What am I supposed to be focusing on?"

Austin gestures his right and left index fingers forward, "Towards the doors. Focus on the anticipation of what might be just on the other side of these doors when the water drains. Think about the love flooding every inch of your soul that will be released onto Luke once you are reunited with him. What happens after that is completely up to you."

A soft ping plays through the confines from overhead.

The squeak of the door opening to the left floors Austin's excitement.

Emily grabs his hand trying to drag him through the small opening already being revealed, but his form does not budge.

She tosses her head over her right shoulder towards him as the smile drains from her face.

He responds to her gesture in a relaxed tone, "We should probably wait until the doors open fully. It might not be stopped completely and I do not want to see you get hurt."

Emily sighs roughly, releasing his hand.

She crosses her arms over her chest in a tight hold, "Why did you have to suggest being in excited mood when I cannot even express it when things like this happen? Now, I am in a bad mood again. Why does nothing ever work out for me?"

Austin releases a slight chuckle, "Emily, right now on your journey you are learning patience. It is obvious from the obstacles that you are being faced with.

You are upset in this elevator because the barriers being presented are testing your patience by preventing you from seeing Luke as soon as you want.

Then I gave you some advice to help in the event that the situation was to ever come up again.

So, the universe changed up the situation just enough to confuse you to see if you learned enough to pass.

If not, you will be given more information in some form or another and keep reliving the same situation where you almost get to the goal, but then it gets pulled out from underneath you.

These *'setbacks'* are not there to destroy you. They are there to build you, but you have to pass the test correctly to be able to move on and see your own progress.

Watch for repetition, any pattern that shows up more than once is a sign, try to acknowledge them more.

The faster you grow, the easier life becomes. Trust me, please. Have I ever misguided you before?"

Emily shakes her head, taking a deep breath. Upon her exhale, they are already walking out of the steel box and into the hallway.

There is nothing to see other than a narrow alley with white walls that are bare in decor and short, rough carpet that ignites the floor into a light gray shade.

Emily finds Austin taking a left, following a small plaque next to the elevator written in dark blue plastic:

←—400-425 | 426-450—→

She nods once to herself in confirmation of his decision as the soles of their shoes shuffle against the rug.

Emily tilts her head to one side then the other as she

dances down the hall to a tune that only she can enjoy. A bright glow radiates from her eyes.

The soft sparkle dims slightly as discomfort rises in her cheeks, "Have you ever smiled so much that your face hurts?"

Austin nods quickly, scanning the doors for identification numbers, "Well, from what I can remember? Only here recently. Why do you ask?"

Emily responds with a relaxed breath, "I do not think I have ever had this experience until now. I always focused so much on my anxiety and impatience. I forgot to give attention to my faith and trust. Without realizing that those two things would destroy a lot of my barriers. Sometimes, since we started going down this journey, I feel stupid for not listening to all of this information a lot sooner. It takes me forever to learn anything."

Austin shakes his head, stopping outside of door 444, "Before we go in there, I want to attempt to offer some help.

Enjoy the good completely. Your problem is not that you are not smart enough to learn the lesson. It is because you are in the process of gaining trust in yourself. In order to do that, you have to first address the reasons why you are not trusting yourself.

However, you do not have to go searching for this answer. I can see it very clearly. You want whatever it is that you are going after, right now or else it floors you with thoughts of betrayal and mistrust. This will then in return place you into a very low vibration.

You do not belong there. You paid your debt, you deserve the best.

All you have to do is slow down and take the time to evaluate all of the details. Do not rush, allow it to play out in Divine timing.

This is the only reason you are not grasping the lessons, if you slow down and apply the proper methods, you will no longer feel like you are stuck.

Free yourself from this, you already know that you are the only one who can."

The sound of footprints heading in their direction from the other side of the door startles them slightly.

An echo of rattling metal bounces through their minds as the heavy, dark stained panel of wood pulls inward.

They both shoot their attention towards the frame to be greeted by the familiar ring of a male's tone, "Guys, I cannot believe this, get in here!"

Emily's mind takes a moment to adjust to the new alterations occurring around her.

Her vision becomes flooded with the image of Luke jogging into her, wrapping her body tightly in a hug.

The smell of falsified leather and pine flood her nose from the splash of cologne smeared against his neck.

Her hands move in a clenching manner trying to gain a firmer hold upon him. Her palms are filled with a light pink, lien suit jacket intertwined with a clump of white cotton from the button down underneath.

Luke releases her from the hold, flashing her a fast grin before dropping his open, right palm towards his leg. He wipes a few loose crumbs onto the side of the matching, pink dress pants.

His line of vision is now glued onto Austin as a growing

grin wraps the right side of his face, "Sorry, I was eating crackers when I heard voices out here in the hall. They were there for a while, so I wanted to investigate."

Austin greets him halfway with open arms.

The smiles on their lips inform me that they feel complete in each other's presence once more.

Luke finally breaks the embrace, "Come on, come in. Sit anywhere you want. Are you hungry?"

Austin feels the tension of his empty stomach spreading into his chest, "Yes. I am starving, thank you."

Luke leads them through the entrance into the main room. The lights are dim. Random, expensive decor is plastered along every inch of the suite. A large, German Shepard pup is hanging the front of his paws over the edge of the cushion, peacefully running through his dreams.

The rest of the couch is being occupied by a random group of well dressed, young men that all seem to radiate privilege. There are two, empty chairs that match the couch directly in front of it, but neither one attempts to claim them.

Emily stares at the men as the room engulfs with Luke's voice that is pulling at her attention, "So, there are bowls of different snacks all throughout the office. If you want something more filling, help yourself to anything that you want in the kitchen. Before you go off and start having fun, I would like to show you the rest of the suite. If that is okay?"

He does not wait for a response. His beaming smile starts to fade as he turns around on his heels without missing a step.

Emily leans her torso forward closing the space between herself and Austin, "Does he seem weird?"

Austin remains silent in thought for a moment, "I think something might be going on, he does seem a little unsettled."

Emily speaks in a harsh whisper, "When are you going to have one of your talks with him, so we can move on and go find Arlenm?"

Austin smiles to himself, before he is given a chance to say anything Luke speaks again, "Back here, where the hall transforms into a T-shape, you can either go right towards the recording studio or left into the bathroom."

Emily tilts her head to the right, "What is the recording studio for?"

A small chuckle slips past his lips, "Tapes, audio books and interviews."

Austin nods his head in interest, "What are the tapes and audios used for?"

Emily does not give him a chance to answer as irritation begins growing within, "And, the interviews?"

A sly grin runs against the right side of his mouth, "Why don't I just show you the room? We can talk more in there. Is it more intimate than being in the hall."

They round the corner at a good pace, their footsteps creak against the floor's structure.
The sound of wood breaking free explodes down the

hall. It does not take long for all of them to enter the studio.

Emily's eyes begin to well with discomfort when she sees that four, young, beautiful women are approaching Luke from different angles with an over-friendly greeting.

Their bodies are covered only in inappropriate places with a lacy, black fabric as they brush against his.

The unknown women can feel the anger flowing off of Emily's form, taking that reaction as their cue to leave. So, they file out of the entrance trying to avoid eye contact Austin and Emily.

Luke turns around slowly to face them. He runs his right hand through his hair as he offers no explanation to anything that is going on.

Emily becomes furious by his silence and rushes at him. She uses both of her palms to shove him back into an empty, office chair that gets shot in reverse from the force of the collision.

The backrest slams into the desk, the recording equipment squeaks upon impact.

His hazy mind is having a difficult time processing what is going on. The only thing he can do is place his head in his right palm and release a small chuckle.

His actions are only adding to the flame that has been lite inside of Emily.

She approaches him with a quick step and a mouth full of swords, "Wait. There is no way I would ever be able to push you over sober. Are you drinking? And, who the hell are those girls? Why are you acting single?"

He does not lift his head as he tries to play his own defense, "No, I am not drinking. I just forgot."

Emily drops to her knees in front of him, hoping to lock eyes, "You forgot what? That you have a girlfriend?"

He shakes his head slowly in sincerity, "I forgot that they were still in here. I am sorry."

Emily tries to hold in the stream of tears rushing past her cheeks, "Who are they and what the hell is going on?"

Before Luke has a chance to conjure up his next reply, she speaks once more, "You know what? I do not even think I want to hear the truth. Whatever you have going on here is more important to you than us. Do you have any idea what me and Austin just went through to get to you? You did not even ask us if we were okay when you saw us. After all of this time that we have been separated and the first thing you want to do is host show and tell? Really?"

She does not give him time to answer, she turns sharply on her heels exiting the room and then out the front door.

Austin takes a deep breath, "I think I need to go check on her right now."

Luke waves his left hand in a swing of irritation towards the entryway.

Austin does not allow too much time to pass before he is also greeted by the stale air in the hall.

His vision falls to the left, where Emily is seated in a crouched position with her knees buried into her chest and her head laying against her arms.

Austin lowers his body into a seated position beside her allowing his legs to extend out in front of his form, "Do you want to talk about it?"

Emily throws her head up slightly, "Talk about what? That Luke has gone rogue and cheated on me in the process?"

A slight laugh flows from Austin's parted lips, "Now, hold on a minute. We do not know for sure yet if that even happened. That is just an opinion at this time."

Emily sighs gently, "Okay, then what am I supposed to do?"

Austin tilts his head to the right, "Go back in there and talk to him about what you are feeling. Try to get some real answers, instead of sitting out here alone in the hallway trying to have a conversation with a person on the other side of the wall."

Emily nods slowly, pulling herself into a full stance.

She leads Austin towards the door. It cracks open to reveal the same, cluttered atmosphere as when they left.

The immediate change they notice is that Luke is now sitting on the couch. The front of his form is hunched over slightly while he crushes some pills against the table. He guides his face forward, snorting the line of blue powder. The chalky coating covers the back of his throat like a thick blanket.

The current energy is shattered by Emily, "Luke, what are you doing?"

Her voice echoes through the space causing everyone,

but Luke to leave the room giving them some alone time.

Austin allows his feet to carry him towards one of the chairs placed in front of Luke.

The guys turn their full interest onto Emily as she begins to lower her form into the seat beside Luke.

Emily holds her gaze steady against the table as tears start to uncontrollably fall, "Why are you doing drugs?"

Luke's eyes widen, "Everyone in this world takes them, it is not that big of a deal. Plus, it was recommended by a friend."

Emily shoves her head down slowly, "So, you are only doing this to help yourself fit in better here in this world or what?"

Luke can sense a slight push of anger flooding the back of his throat, "You do not know what you are talking about. If you came here just to judge me and get me out of this then leave. I do not care. I am quitting the game. I have decided that I want to live out the rest of my physical existence here in this world."

Emily takes a sharp breath, she tries to speak, but no words are released as she storms out of the front door.

Luke takes a long drink out of a clear crystal with a caramel-colored liquid splashing against the sides.

He is so focused on himself in this moment, that he does not even realize that Austin has passed him to chase after Emily.

Austin does not have to look far to find her, she is

against the wall of the hallway in a defeated placement once again.

He crouches down in front of her using his hands to sturdy his weight, "What are you thinking? What do you want to do?"

Emily speaks in a painful wail, "I do not know what to do anymore. I mean, what the hell is even happening?"

Austin exhales slowly, "I know that right now this is really hard, but you only have two options that will put both of you in the safest situation.
Option one: You leave him here and allow him to destroy himself with no chance.
Option two: You can go back in there with me, wait until he hits rock bottom then drag him out at that point when he is ready.
Which one do you want to do?"

Emily allows a small whisper to escape her chest, "Option two, but I do not know how long the new me will be able to hold on to something that is destroying me."

Austin nods slowly with a growing grin of approval of her thoughts, "Okay, let's go. If this is what you want, stay strong. If not, you are always free to leave."

Emily feels the gelatin-like substance of her legs under her weight, "I hope we are not too late to save him."

Before Austin has a chance to respond, a loud clash of something fragile breaking, rings through the space.

He pushes Emily backwards slightly with silent hand gestures, making sure they stay as unnoticeable as possible.
Emily exhales in annoyance, "You were never planning

on forcing him to leave, were you?"

Austin licks his bottom lip softly, "No. We cannot make him do something he does not want to do, but I do not want you to leave this building with regrets, regardless of what choice he makes for himself."

Without giving her a chance to process the statement, he turns his head over his left shoulder, seeing all of the people from inside leaving the room in a single file line of rage.

He turns his focus against Emily, "To answer your previous question, I think we got here at the perfect time."

They take a deep breath before walking back inside to find that Luke is sitting on the couch in what appears to be a sleeping position.

Emily looks at Austin with concern. He nods once in confirmation before leading her forward.

Austin leans the upper-half of his form forward when he reaches Luke, "Are you asleep?"

Luke shakes his head, "Just enjoying the high."

Austin nods once in understanding, "Do you think you could tell us what is going on now that everyone else is gone?"

Luke shakes his head slowly.

Austin exhales deeply, "Well, we are all you have left. So, if you want to get out of this situation. You have to tell me before me and Emily continue on."

Luke slowly opens his left eye, pushing his weight into a straighter position, "You would really leave me?"

Austin pushes his head forward in one, firm motion, "We love you enough to stay, but we love ourselves enough to leave. The best thing for us as a group is not to stay here, it is to go on to find something better. If you do not want to leave, we understand. However, never mistake your fear with our lack of love."

His chest decompresses slowly, "Okay, I will tell you. When Dalton first took me, he wanted to use the information for himself. Then, after we started talking more and he heard what I had to say, he wanted me to help everyone. We made tapes, they started selling like crazy. It was amazing to watch all of the money come in. I did not think it would be a problem, but then everything started to change. I spiraled out of control, I could not help it. Waking up that morning with nothing and then going to bed with everything I ever wanted was a lot to process and I did not give myself the time I needed to readjust.

Now, I am so far into this mess, I do not know if I will ever be able to get out."

Austin flashes him a fast grin of hope, "You will do what you have to do because it is the best thing for you."

Luke shakes his head, "I do not know what is best for me. I always thought that if I had money, it would give me enough pride to seal my pain. All it did was make me turn into a complete jerk. I should have been out there looking for you guys, instead of sitting in here enjoying my life."

Austin tilts his facial structure to the left, "Was it fun?"

Luke shrugs slowly, "No. I tried to have fun, but every time I am messed up, I have really horrible experiences inside. It is more anxiety than excitement."

Austin nods slowly, "So, does this mean that you have had enough of the high life? Are you ready to go with us to find Arlenm?"

The air between them shifts, "No. I cannot leave, yet. I am not ready."

Emily attempts to hold back her feelings, "Did you sleep with those women? Are they the reason you want to stay?"

Luke squints his brows sharply, "No. I did not sleep with them. We have them in promotional pieces to boost sales. They are so friendly with me because I was the one who suggested to Dalton that they needed a raise. They got enough to help them transition. Trust me, I would be thankful, too."

Emily is too busy processing the relief flowing through her veins to ask any further questions.

Austin clears his throat gently, "What do you mean, *transitioning*? Into what?"

Luke takes a deep inhale trying to alleviate the pounding tension running through his temples, "In this world all of the *poor* people are half-human and half-creature. Only when you have enough money, do you become complete in a physical sense with no more social restraints."

Austin inhales slowly, "Is Dalton not rich? He runs the whole world, why is he part creature?"

Luke is becoming visibly irritated under the drugs, "Just because this is his world, does not mean that he is exempt to any of the rules. In fact, they are forced much harder on him due to him also being the world's influence.

However, being the ruler of the world does not come with as big of a check as one might think.

That is why we went into business together, I wanted to help him achieve his dream. I just did not realize one of my own was being built around me until it was too late."

Austin nods his head slowly trying to finish processing what has just been said, "Do you feel any different since before you were kidnapped to, now?"

Luke is unsure of what he is referring to and does not want to just assume, "What do you mean? Different how?"

Emily jumps into the conversation, "Emotionally, mentally or spiritually?"

Luke runs his right, cuffed hand over his mouth, "Yes. I guess, I have noticed that a few things seem different. Like, I suddenly feel more aware of myself and other people. I keep getting more and more information downloaded into my mind. It is useful to me and a lot of others. Outside of that and all the money, not much else has changed."

Emily rolls her eyes slightly in annoyance, "And, your hair."

Luke leans his torso forward, "Do you not like it?"

She allows her vision to jump in an upwards motion, scanning over the longer, pushed back strands on the top that gently fade into a short buzz on the side and in the back.

She drops her gaze towards the table, "It is cute."

Luke pushes his weight backwards into a defeated, lounging placement, tilting his attention towards Austin,

"Man, why is she so mad at me?"

Austin allows his gaze to catch against Luke's, "She is upset that the intelligent, sweet man she fell in love with is getting all of this wonderful information to save the world, yet is failing when it comes to serving himself."

Luke hangs his head forward, "I do not know why I cannot let it go."

Austin nods once in understanding, "You do know why, you just do not want to allow it to come back to the surface because you fear it. That is why you are trying to destroy it with drugs."

A loud, unknown pound upon the door of the suite causes all of their attention to shoot towards the closed entry.

Luke pulls himself to his feet, mumbling under his breath, "Now, what?"

Luke opens the door to see that Kave is filling the entrance.

A large smile runs against Luke's lips, "What are you doing here? Is everything okay?"

Kave nods once in a firm manner, "I am here to inform you guys that we are twenty minutes outside of the shore. I need all of you to please gather your things and come with me back to the ship. The Captain would like to have a word with you before your departure."

Austin and Emily rush to the exit upon hearing this information.

Emily squeezes past Kave, stumbling into the hall with a large wave of grief surrounding her.

Austin follows closely behind, patting Luke on the back in passing, "Come on, it is time to go."

Luke shakes his head slowly, "I told you. I cannot go."

CHAPTER THIRTY-SEVEN:

Austin flashes him a fast smile, "You have to stay authentic to yourself. Only you know what is best for you. It is not our job to change you. Our job is to love you until you decide to change for yourself. However, we expect the same respect back. We have to go because that is the best thing for us. We want you to come with us, but if your happiness is not with us then we cannot ask you to give all of this up and follow."

Kave gently lays his right palm on Austin's shoulder, "We have ten minutes. We can still make it, but we have to go right now. I apologize for the rush."

Austin only nods once in response, he turns his attention towards Luke, "I understand."

Kave and Austin back away from the entrance that Luke is leaning the left side of his body against.

Luke's eyes widen sharply as he pushes the front of his form forward. He peers down the left side of the hall to see that Emily is nowhere in sight.

He tries to hold down a growing anxiety creeping into his mind, *I cannot believe that she left me. She did not even say goodbye.'*

I do not stay in the dark room with Luke. My excitement is too high. I have to find my pawns, knowing they are closer than ever to freeing me makes my emotions sail in a positive vibration.

They are just now climbing back through the wave and

onto the boat.

The molecules pinch themselves together tightly, creating a transparent bridge to escort them between the gap of reality and dreams.

I exhale with a soothing relief when the sound of their soles smack against the wooden floor of the deck.

Their vision snags against the Captain, who is patiently awaiting their arrival.

She greets them both with a sincere smile, "I am glad to hear that you found Luke. I apologize it did not go the way you wanted."

Emily can feel the fear and reality of what just happened fully sinking in.

Her attention rests firmly on the Captain, "Maybe, you could go talk to him."

The Captain shakes her head slowly, "I am sorry. I cannot assist him against his will. He has to want the help. Otherwise, he will not hear a word I say and it will just be a waste of his time."

A line of pain runs off of her eyes, "Okay."

Emily checks herself out of the conversation and into the confines of her mind.

The Captain shifts her attention onto Austin, "You are doing the right thing."

Austin grins softly, "You said to always be authentic, even if no one else can understand why you are doing it."

The Captain nods slowly, "If they use their information like a shovel, it will dig them out of this hole. If the only thing preventing him from being free is putting it into action. You did your part, the rest is up to him."

She tilts her head to the left, "Who are you?"

Austin nods once, thinking over the answer to himself before carelessly releasing it into the air, "I am here to free people from a cage they did not even realize they were prisoner to. I am everything and nothing all at the same time. I am shapeless and formless. Allowing me to be anything that I need to be at any time."

A prideful grin glides against the Captain's mouth as they nod once in silence to each other before Austin turns his attention onto Emily.

He takes her hand inside of his, leading her towards the front of the boat.

Austin tries to tame her mind, "Isn't this great? I remember when we were running towards the portal the first few times, not knowing if we were going to survive or not. It has gotten much better. Look at us, we are just casually approaching the next adventure."

Emily turns her head over the structure of her right shoulder as she scans the area hoping for a sign from Luke, "Or, a nightmare."

CHAPTER THIRTY-EIGHT:

I watch in a whirl of amusement as Austin and Emily barge through the portal, entering the black void between the two worlds.

For the first time since they entered my game, they do not show fear in this capsule.

They both stand with their arms behind their backs and their feet positioned a foot apart in a sturdy stance.

A sly grin runs against the right side of Austin's mouth as he awaits the next challenge with excitement.

The empty echo of rubber hitting against the tilted floor of my mind rings through the space, demanding their full attention.

The figure steps out of the shadow to reveal himself in the dim overhead lighting as Master Brutus.

He matches their enthusiasm, "I thought for sure you would not complete the class, but you did. I swore that you would not learn how to apply it to your reality, but you are. I bet money, that you would not be strong enough by time you reached Luke to leave him behind, but I lost.
I am starting to understand why Arlenm went insane. You are a lot stronger than any humans we have ever encountered before."

Austin nods his head processing his response, "We are not stronger, we just could not settle for empty tomorrows. We knew there had to be more and we were determined to find it. It is not strength that leads you towards higher ground, its love."

Master Brutus feels a drain of negative energy leak from his chest in their presence, "Well then, I guess you are more than ready to complete the final test. It is going to put you into situations unlike any you have ever experienced before. You will be given as much help as you decide to let yourself receive. The world will speak to you, that and your inner trust is the only map you will receive.

If you pass, you will not only save Arlenm, but you have the possibility to free yourself. Whatever tries to destroy you out there, make sure one of your enemies is not yourself.

With all of that being discussed, it is here that I wish you the best of luck.

Welcome to the last world in the land of Arlenm.

You have earned this spot. Now, let's see if you gain another shot at your lives when this is all over."

Master Brutus does not allow his voice to fully fade from the room before he snaps the fingers of his left hand.

The illusion of four, identical, black walls are knocked down around them as if the force of Master Brutus' gesture was that intense.

The structures collapse onto the ground, kicking up a huge cloud of gray dust to surround the area.

Austin waves his right hand in front of his face trying to prevent him from breathing in mounds of rock.

Before he gets a fair chance to evaluate their surroundings his ears become flooded with Emily's frantic vibration, "Austin, I really need you right now."

He nods his head once in understanding, closing the space between them, "What are you experiencing?"

Tears uncontrollably stream down the sides of her face,

"I honestly do not know. I have never felt this horrible. It feels like someone is sticking their hands inside of my chest and pulling my heart and lungs into a million, tiny pieces. I am not sure if I want to be alone or ask you to hug me, until I start to once again feel whole. I do not know if I want to laugh about what just happened or break down into a fit of agony knowing that I just walked out on the one person in the entire world who never would have left me."

Austin places his right hand gently on top of her shoulder, "You did not make a mistake. Your guides would have never allowed that to happen. Plus, you did not walk out on him. He walked out on himself. All you did was decide that you could no longer sit and watch him sink deeper because you knew that if you stayed around long enough, you would have abandoned yourself, too."

Emily tries to offer a response through rough gasps of air, "Austin, to be honest. At this point, I do not know what I believe in anymore."

Austin tilts his head to the left, "What do you mean?"

Emily can feel the weight of her doubt beginning to press against the inner confines of her chest, "Sometimes, it is hard for me to believe that any of the stuff that the Captain said is even true. Not because I do not want to believe it. Trust me, I want nothing more in this world than to have a strong connection to the Divine, complete understanding and inner peace.
I do not know. I am having a hard time because I am unsure what is true or not."

Austin nods slowly trying to evaluate her current placement beyond what she is able to express, "Emily."

He pauses gently attempting to add a more relaxed vibe

to the conversation, "No matter which direction you are going to go down, one thing you cannot deny is accepting that there is a higher power.

There is way too many things that happened in my life, in your life, in every person in existences life, that were done so perfectly and so thought out, there is no other explanation."

Emily shrugs her shoulders, "At this moment, my mind cannot recall any."

A fast laugh slips past his lips, "You cannot remember because your mind is like your best friend. When you have an opinion about something whether it is good, bad, right or wrong. Your mind is going to support you in whichever direction you decide to go.

For instance, you in this moment, do not want to believe in the higher power, so your brain constructs evidence to back that theory by blocking the magic from your memory as well as the current reality that you are living in. If you want to see the magic, you first have to accept that it is there."

Emily exhales slowly allowing the breath to trickle against her bottom lip, "What happened that made you start to feel this change within yourself?"

His vision darts towards the scattering grains of sand being illuminated by the pale moon light, "The minute I started to find answers. It made me want to live, but just remaining on the physical was never and still is not enough for me. It made me want to wake up in a world that is so happy, all of the pain I ever felt would just be a distant fragment of the past. It made me want to find a girl, who will love me so deeply, I forget what it felt like when I used to settle for any lesser definition of the word. It made me want to ride the waves instead of gasping for air at the water's edge. It locked me into an unbreakable search for more."

Emily swallows violently trying to push her emotions back down, "How do you feel now?"

He allows the weight of his head to fall to the left, "I am so glad this is my life, but most importantly, I have never felt freer."

Emily throws her arms over her head in a dramatic response, "For what? Who cares if you feel alive? We are literally in a game with one way out, death. The last thing I feel right now is freedom. So, if this is the end, what was the point of everything you went through? Everything that I went through. What about Raven, Luke, Nash and Morgan? What about all of their suffering and pain?"

Austin shakes his head with a goofy grin plastered against his face, "Em, I cannot speak for anyone else, not even you. However, on behalf of myself, all I have to say is, this is the adventure I am glad I lived for. We were kidnapped and put into a game that I could not have created in my wildest dreams. If you were to ask me, it has been one pretty awesome story. No matter how it ends, I am glad I got to be a part of it."

All of the anger inside of her form begins to melt into the currents of the wind.

A nervous laugh floods the air, "You are right. I guess, this whole thing is pretty cool."

CHAPTER THIRTY-NINE:

Austin does not allow the smirk on his lips to fade, "Now, we have a whole other adventure awaiting us yet in this world. There is nothing in this moment that I would desire more than for you to be able to enjoy this experience with me. So, are you ready for the transition to start or do you still want to stay where you are? I mean, it is completely up to you. I am in no rush."

She flashes her vision towards him, examining the calming energy that surrounds his figure, "Okay, I give up. I cannot keep fighting it anymore. Being stuck in the middle of transitioning is literally destroying me mentally, emotionally and physically."

Austin's mouth breaks into a full-sized grin, "Then you are just going to have to trust me and yourself enough to dive right in."

Emily cannot offer any form of response outside of nodding her head.

Austin does not allow another second of silence to pass by, "Okay, when we were in the classroom, how much of what the Captain said actually stuck with you?"

Emily inhales sharply, "I guess, not as much as I first assumed. I cannot believe we are going to have a conversation about self-help to better explain to me how self-help works. I feel like a really big idiot, right now."

Austin can feel the currents of energy flowing off of her form, cracking into his, "Do not feel that way. Everyone processes things differently and maybe at the time, you were not able to hear the Captain for the same reason she could not go talk Luke out of his mess. Maybe, you just were not ready."

She cannot hold down a burst of emotion racing up the back of her throat, "What makes you think I am ready now?"

He allows the end of his tongue to graze against his bottom lip, "You just went through some pretty heavy stuff with Luke."

She rolls her eyes sharply at his response, "What does that have to do with anything?"

Austin tips his head back slightly, "Every time you are destroyed, you are given the chance to redo the entire project that is you. Try not to fight situations that will allow your growth. You will by nature shift whether you try or not."

Emily tilts her head down attempting to hide the tears that are starting to sting the back of her eyes, "If everything is going to change anyway then what the hell is the point? Why are we even doing this?"

His positive vibration does not waiver in the face of her fear, "Things will change regardless of whether you do the work or not. The amount of effort you put in, determines if the change will be good or bad. Either way, everything this time tomorrow will be completely different."

Emily smiles briefly, "You are right. Something good has to come out of all this."

Austin nods once in a firm manner, "Great, then all you have to do is free yourself from your own restraints. There are a lot of things that are going to be against you in life, do not be one of them. I know the Captain said the same thing a lot throughout the class, but it is so important. You can be the only thing standing between yourself and being complete without ever even realizing it.

Please, if you can try to avoid this as much as possible. I held myself back from things, we both have. We did that for too long, it is time to stop being afraid."

Emily exhales slowly trying to sort through the files of her mind, "Okay, what do you think I should do? I do not even know where to start. My brain is a jumbled mess of nonsense."

A light chuckle slips from his mouth.

Her head shifts sharply in his direction, "Austin, this is not funny."

Austin brings his mouth into a half-sided grin, "It is not funny that you are going through this but learning to laugh at your problems, makes them appear less frightening. The first thing you have to stop doing is looking at every change as an end. It would be like driving down a path until it ends, leaving you with two new options right or left. You not wanting to take either option or just sitting at the end of the road for the rest of your life would drive you crazy and you would eventually want to go somewhere else. There is no destination in life, do not look for an end because you will be searching for the rest of your time in this physical plane.

Figure out what you need to do or have in order to survive the journey as comfortably as possible. When you are thinking about this, look inside of yourself for answers before you start looking out. Things that are on the outside of you can be and should be used, but never to build the foundation of who you are. This is what you should be focusing on."

Emily can feel her mind beginning to come to life under his words, "I do not know what I need. Can you tell me what you are seeing that I still need to work on? Please."

Austin pushes his head forward, "You have to deal with what just happened with Luke, like I said it is a pretty big thing you just went through.

Em, if we were back on Earth and this same situation happened to you there, what would your friends and family tell you to do? What kind of advice would they offer?"

She tilts her head to the left, getting lost in the endless void of sand dunes, "They would more than likely say that he is a jerk. I deserve better. I need to just get on with my life and forget that I was ever with him. They will say that he just loved his addictions more than he ever loved me."

The wheels of her mind continue to play through the different scenarios, but her mouth falls still.

Austin clears his throat sharply, hoping to break the silence, "How do you feel about that advice?"

Emily shrugs her shoulders slowly, "I do not know. I feel like it might not be the best way to handle the situation. I mean, if I take their advice, all I am doing is hiding the fact that it ever happened and it could work for a while as long as I am single, it will be fine. I can push it away, forget about him and just move on.

However, I will eventually think that I am strong enough to enter into another relationship, but the minute I do, it will all come flooding back of how not so okay I truly am. Then it will flow through every inch of my new relationship. I do not want that for me, Luke or someone else."

Austin scoots his figure closer to her, "Maybe, I have a perspective that might make things clearer. I would not suggest taking that advice. The first thing you have to do is accept the changes that occurred to construct this new reality.

Spend some time in it, look at it from different angles, keep searching until you can come to peace with the way things are now. I would try not to spend too much time here. Once you feel like you are good with this area, move onto the next. Which will involve you forgiving him and releasing any negative energy that you associate with Luke or the situation.

I know that this is the hardest part, but you have to do it. There really is no other way around it.

When that part is over, you are going to want to start building a new path for yourself that no longer revolves around Luke. Re-evaluate what you want. Then when you are going through this phase of construction, start making all new, positive actions towards where you want to be in all areas of your life. You might be forced to go out of your comfort zone for a while during this process, but it is normal and needed. Do not leave this part out. Otherwise, you will not see the results that you want and feel like you are getting nowhere."

A small pause forms between them.

Austin pushes the direction of the conversation onto her, "What are you thinking? Is this avenue more of your cup of tea?"

She cannot help but to release a small laugh at his word choice, "Yes, it is. Thanks, Austin."

Austin tips his head back slightly, "Emily, it is not true. You know that, right?"

Her eyebrows squint sharply, "What is not true?"

Austin grins, using only the left side of his mouth, "That Luke loved drugs more than you. He also is not a jerk. He is just going through some problems within himself. He thinks that drugs are the answer to make him feel whole."

A small stream of tears is running down her cheek, "Why was I not enough to make him feel complete?"

Austin tilts his head to the left, "Love does not fix people. Love can only truly exist when both people are already healed. It is not a glue to hold you together, but rather a reward for the work you did to get there. Love can only be appreciated when you truly understand what the word itself means. This goes beyond just relationships, leaking its way into love as a whole.

Only the strongest souls can love unconditionally after being completely shattered. I know that you are one of them."

CHAPTER FORTY:

While Emily begins the process of sorting out her mental and emotional state, Austin allows his focus to be given to the next task, finding me.

His voice comes to life, "Do you need more time or do you think you are ready to head towards Arlenm?"

Emily slowly nods, "I think we can go. I mean, if I need a break from something, I will just let you take over for a while. I do not like the idea of just sitting here wasting time when we are so close to being able to go home."

Austin exhales loudly, "It is never a waste of time to take care of yourself. If you do not do it now, you will be forced to do it later."

Emily flashes him a fast grin, lifting the pitch of her voice, "Or, I could do it on the way as long as you do not mind if I need a rest."

He pushes his lips together tightly in a thinking manner, "Okay, but only because the excitement of being where we are is really intense and I do not think that I will be able to sit still for a couple more hours myself."

She nods her head once in an unenthusiastic sway.

He pulls all of his weight into a vertical placement before reaching his hands down to offer her a boost in the right direction.

Now, that they are both on their feet, Austin turns his head to the left, "Come on, let's go check out that sign over there."

Emily nods her head once in agreement.

While Austin walks, his head falls towards the unknown that stretches out for miles all around them. It brings a high energy to be exerted through his stride.

He approaches the back of the sign examining the metal plate with a white, rectangular sticker sitting on the bottom, left corner.

His eyes quickly scan the object, "I think we should head into the desert. The bar code has the number two hundred and twenty-two hidden in the middle. This is a sign that we are on the right path."

He is unable to see her reaction because she is lost in thought as she evaluates the other side, "Well, we have a problem then because the number two hundred and twenty-two is on this side as well. However, it is facing the city. So, which direction should we head?"

Austin raises his right hand towards his face, "Probably towards the desert since it is the direction of the first green light we received."

Emily does not respond verbally to his decision. She only feels her legs being dragged by her defeated form.

Austin does not allow the silence to consume them any longer, "How are you doing back there? What has been going through your head?"

Her eyes roll slowly in annoyance, "Is this going to be a new thing? You constantly asking me how I am feeling."

Austin laughs slightly before processing his next thought, "Your first thought of my actions was negative because you do not want to feel like I think I am better than you, which I do not. I am asking as often as I am because I understand that the constant shift of emotions that overcome you when a trauma hits can be hard to deal with on your own and during that time, it is common to need a lot of reassurance. Basically, I am going in a roundabout way of saying, if you need to talk about something, even if it is the same thing a hundred times because you need to hear a hundred different ways, I will not get upset with you."

A small mass of energy releases from her chest, "You know there is nothing that annoys me more than when I am angry at someone and they respond by being calm. I used to hate when Luke did that, it made me feel like he was not taking the situation seriously."

Austin holds on tight to his smile, "Do you ever feel silly after getting angry about a situation?"

She swallows roughly, her discomfort with the question rings through the air, "Yes."

Austin nods slowly in understanding, "Then why are you upset that I do not want to hurt myself or others by losing control of my emotions? I do not want to carry that guilt or make others engulf in pain. It is not that I do not care because I do. I just do not believe any obstacle is so severe, I have to hurt someone else because it is harming me in that moment."

Emily closes her eyes tightly with disappointment in herself for not realizing this sooner, "I really do not even know why I reacted that way all of those times. Looking back on the situations now, I notice that I was not even feeling anger half of the time. It was kind of like I was just playing through the motions of what I felt like I was supposed to be doing. I do not know what I can do to fix it."

Austin slows his speed slightly, closing the space between them, "You react the way you think you should or what society says you should do because when you act out of what is considered *normal,* you are shamed for it.

You just yelled at me for not being mad at you. Not because you secretly want me to be upset, but you were frustrated with me because you could not understand how I was able to do it.

However, whether you see it right now or not, this is a good thing.

Just because we have a little more insight onto what is going on, does not mean that there is not a whole lot left to learn. Do not ever stop looking for better ways to improve on yourself. Sometimes our biggest teachers are the way other people treat us when they show love. Not to make us feel like we are less than them, but to show us the possibility of who we can become."

Emily feels her eyes widen sharply under this new bit of knowledge, "I think I missed out on a lot of those lessons."

Austin runs his left hand through the strands of his hair, "Do not worry about it. If you are meant to learn it along the journey, the right information will come to you at the perfect time. Much like anger, stress is also an emotion that serves no purpose towards yourself or others. Get rid of it. Trust is what you need the most to relax. Thankfully for you, the chair is already built all you have to do is sit down."

Emily slowly exhales, "I am having a hard time fully fitting into a path that leads to the Divine. I feel confused and it bothers me when I feel this way. I want a relationship with the Divine so desperately I would do anything, yet nothing fully sits right with me. What do I do?"

Austin ensures that she is okay by offering a nudge of laughter, "Not everyone will be comfortable making this switch and some might even feel confused on what the right thing to think is. If you are feeling this way, create your own path."

Emily squints her eyes sharply, "How can I follow my own path? I want to follow the path of the Divine."

Austin releases a gentle smile, "Do you believe in love?"

Emily nods quickly, "Yes, of course."

Austin inhales slowly, "Then start there. Love is your new path until you find something that is already or will be created that better suits you. Practice it towards yourself and everything else in existence. Giving and receiving love unconditionally. That is where you start right now. if nothing else in this moment feels secure."

Emily can feel desperation hanging against her words, "I do not understand how doing this will bring me closer to the Divine."

Austin stares up gently towards the gorgeous skyline, "No matter where the path of love takes you, all paths of unconditional love flow back to the Divine. If you live a life of love, you will find the Divine along the path."

Emily drops her head down slightly, a loud inhale of clogged nasal passages ring against the air.

He tilts his head sharply, "What is wrong? Why are you crying?"

Emily shrugs her shoulders, "I don't know. I guess, it still hurts about Luke. I feel so guilty for just leaving him like that. I know you said it was the best thing for all of us, but I am still trying to see through the illusions of that truth."

Austin nods slowly, "Can I ask you something? If you were Luke, right now and he was in your situation. Knowing what you know about your journey this far. What would you say to him if the tables were reversed? How would you want him to react? Remember, this advice has to come solely from a place of love. What are you going to say to him?"

Emily swallows roughly, she can feel the words scraping against the back of her throat, "I would tell him to live his life full of love, a love so strong it could heal the entire world. I would tell him to be free from the burdens and chains I have placed upon him throughout the years. I would tell him to continue on for me, not to look at it as living without me. I would want him to complete every dream we ever shared and fill the list with many more. I would tell him to be happy, to be free."

Austin pushes his head forward, "Then that is exactly what you need to do."

CHAPTER FORTY-ONE:

They find themselves still heading through the vacant lands.

My mind is brought to life by distant laughter, every step they take in my direction causes anxiety to race through my form.

My neck strains in an upwards motion, looking out of the small, tinted window of the steel capsule that my physical form is currently locked inside of.

I want to know more about what my humans are doing. I try to leave my fleshy figure, but freedom is the furthest thing from what I achieve.

A shot of frustration flies from my chest as my body tenses, "Why can I not leave my body?"

The veins protruding out from underneath my skin pulses from the rage that is now bouncing through my mind.

A soft, three-note knock of an index finger captures my interest.

My eyes strain towards the window as I stretch my body forward trying to get a better look at who is nudging for my attention.

The smeared, reflective surface becomes clouded with the image of Master Brutus' smug smile beaming through me.

An irritated line is thrown from my lips, "What do you want?"

Master Brutus pushes his mouth into a forced frown, "You had a question for me, right?"

My head tilts to the left sharply, "No. I do not."

Master Brutus tries his hardest to hold down a smirk, "Oh, hmm. That is weird because I could have sworn that you asked why you were trapped inside of your body."

A deep growl escapes my chest, "Okay, fine. Why am I trapped in my body, Brutus?"

His lips push together tightly in surprise, "I have not heard you call me that in years. What happened to the respect you once had for me?"

I try to ignore my pain by laughing in a forced bark, "I lost that when you betrayed me."

His energy shifts to a softer tone, "Betray you? I never once betrayed you. You did this to yourself. How can you even blame me? You were the one who failed at being a game leader. So, I decided to help you by showing you how a real champion runs a show."

Master Brutus pauses slightly, hitting his open, right palm against the side of the metal prison, "Get ready, Arlenm. The only way to learn is to go in. You have just become a pawn in my game."

A fist of air is stolen from my chest as his words collide against my ears.

Before I am given a moment to process the reality of what just happened and offer a response, he vanishes from my sight.

Seeing him disappear causes an uncontrollable rage to throw my body into a fit of agony.

My limbs smash into the walls of the capsule, I feel the vibration from the impact coursing through my form, but no pain runs against my nerves.

A single thought rushes into my mind, 'What the hell is going on with me?'

The idea of something being abnormal inside of me causes a dark energy to start creeping into my form.

I quickly channel my thoughts in a different direction not wanting to deal with such negativity, 'Where is Austin and Emily? They need to get me out of here, so I can take back my game.'

I am forced to use only my sense to pick up on their energy frequency.

They appear to be around one-hundred-feet away. It seems like they are heading in the right direction, thankfully.

This knowledge only relieves me slightly. Hardly any time passes before a slight ringing courses through my ears.

It is Austin, "Okay, Emily this is good. Another sign, it says there is a town up ahead four-hundred and forty-four miles away."

Emily's tone sparks with slight excitement, "Great. What does that mean? Are we still going in the right direction?"

Austin nods his head, "It means that we have backing from the spirit world."

Her eyes widen in amusement as she directs her attention towards the path.

I can feel the negative vibrations flowing through my legs as my right foot taps violently against the floor panels.

I drag my right palm in a slow motion down my face, "If they do not get me out of here in the next five minutes, I am going to lose my mind!"

Suddenly, I hear the soft ping of an alarm bouncing through my brain.

Before I have a good chance to wrap my thoughts around the source of the beeping, a shadowy figure passes by the window, snagging my attention.

I quickly react by pressing my palms against the flesh of the cool glass, "Hey! Who are you?"

A fast smear of colors rise into my sight as Austin's head starts coming into focus.

His whisper snags against the back of his throat, "Arlenm? Are you in there?"

I try to refrain from releasing any negative emotions, but I can feel some beginning to slip out, "Yes. Can you open the door?"

A small pause of tension rises between us, "It looks like there is some kind of a code we have to figure out."

A breath of annoyance is forced from my lungs, "Can you try to pry it open?"

Austin shakes his head quickly, "It is sealed shut. There is no sense in even trying that."

I can no longer contain my frustration. I slam my palms against the reflective surface, it trembles in response.

Austin remains calm, "Do you have any idea what the code might be?"

All of the sudden, for a reason that is unknown to me, everything around me slowly starts to fade from my hearing, even the mumble of Austin's fading tone.

The only thing I am able to capture is the gentle call of the alarm that is still ringing.

My head snaps sharply in Austin's direction, "Hey, you and Emily try to figure out where that alarm is coming from."

Austin grins slightly, using only the right side of his mouth, "I thought you wanted me to free you?"

A harsh growl leaves my tongue, "I want you to go find the reason for the alarm, now! This is important! I am part of the game now, too. Master Brutus has never had a human make it this far in one of the games. That is why he is the best game leader in history. Those alarms could be from motion detectors coming from somewhere in the surrounding area. If they are alarms, that means someone is being sent here to kill us. Now, go look!"

Austin reacts to my hysteria by gently nodding his head with a sot grin, "It is alright. Everything is good. I will go check. I will be right back, do not move."

Before he vanishes from my sight, he shoots me a fast wink with his left eye.

My vision widens in response as I mumble to myself, "What the hell is wrong with that kid? He really has no fear now?"

The corner of my right eye catches against the dragging form of Emily in front of me.

My body lunges forward towards the barrier, "Emily! Hey! Come here!"

Her interest peeks under the muffled echo of her name.

She slowly pulls herself in my direction.

My jaw unintentionally clenches under her lack of compassion for my current situation.

Finally, she is close enough that I do not have to strain my voice in an attempt to communicate, "Austin had to go do something. Can you help me try to figure out the code until he gets back?"

Emily nods her head slowly, "Okay, what do you think it is"

Excitement floods my tone, "Hmm. Try my birthday."

She tilts her head to the left, "And, how am I supposed to know that? We are not exactly friends, remember?"

I lean my face closer to the glass, my lips graze against the surface as I speak, "Now, is not the time to be a—"

My mind blanks on the insult as I catch a hold of her eyes, "Just go to the keypad and type."

She exhales sharply through her nose as she leans the front half of her form forward, "What is it?"

I feel like I cannot unleash the information fast enough, "17-21-0002."

Emily squints sharply, "That is the most bizarre birthday ever."

I pull my shoulders back slightly, "Did it work?"

Emily glances down in an unenthusiastic sway, "Uh, no. The light is still flashing red. Do you have any other options? I could just try random number combinations if you want."

My voice cracks against the air, "He would not make a security code something so simplistic and stupid. It has to mean something important to him."

Before she has a chance to respond, Austin's footsteps break into our surroundings.

By time he reaches us, he is out of breath, "Hey, guys. There were some motion detectors that got set off back there."

Without knowing if he was finished with his information, words begin to leak from my mind, "Did you see anything coming this way when you were looking for the alarms?"

Austin crosses his arms over his chest, "No which means that we still have plenty of time. There is no reason to panic."

I toss my vision to glance around his form, the glossy surface of my vision reflects the image of something heading this way.

My bottom lip falls down slightly, "What the hell is that?"

CHAPTER FORTY-TWO:

Austin and Emily turn around to see a large, dark mass moving towards them at a fast speed along the sky way.

Austin tilts his head over his left shoulder towards Emily, "I do not think we have much time."

Emily throws her vision onto the keypad, "Arlenm, what is another code?"

The pressure that is currently being directed on me to find a solution to the chaos unfolding quickly around us is causing sweat to begin leaking from my hairline.

I exhale in a choppy breath, "Okay. Try this 09-03-0000."

Emily nods her head quickly. It would feel to her as if she cannot make her fingers move fast enough.

The sound of eight, faint clicks scrape against my ears as anxiety engulfs my figure, "What is happening now?"

I immediately can tell by the delay of response that the outcome is not currently playing out in my favor.

My tightly closed fists slam into the glossy flesh.

Emily's voice cracks against the uncertainty hanging in the air, "It says that we only have one attempt left."

Her attention turns in the opposite direction to see that the overhead shadow is now much closer than she had hoped.

She allows the tip of her tongue to glide against her

bottom lip, "Okay, what is something else that you think it could be?"

A silence falls over us as I begin scanning my brain in search of something structural to build off of.

My racing mind is cut in half by Emily's frantic tone, "Arlenm, now!"

My words stretch across the air currents in a broken, fragile state, "How am I supposed to think, when you are screaming at me?"

Before she has a moment to respond, something slams against the top of the capsule.

A shiver of vibration runs through my body and the structure.

It does not take me long to regain my inner balance.

I slam my right palm against the glass, "What was that?"

Austin's from appears in my vision from a crouching position, "It fell from the cloud, part of it is still overhead."

My eyes widen in fear under this knowledge, "What is it?"

Austin shrugs looking over the small, orange sphere that is now half buried in the sand, "It is a metal ball with a timer counting down from five minutes and two seconds."

He turns his attention onto the surroundings, "That cloud is still above us. It is dropping the explosives all around us."

Emily lifts her head towards me, "Okay, Arlenm. Think. What is the most important thing to Master Brutus?"

The words fall from my mouth with no filter, "I thought it was me."

My mind starts to reply her previous question through my brain on repeat.

Suddenly, my eyes widen as I shoot my form forward, speaking in a breathless sway, "I know what it is. Try 15-05-0025."

Emily's face contours into a serious vibe as she quickly punches in the code.

A bright, green light appears in the structure of a small square. The metal cracks as the panel is released from the frame.

I waste no time removing myself from the capsule. My first breath of freedom is smooth and deep.

Austin is now able to pick up on my energy.

He crosses his arms over his chest gently, "What was it?"

I release a long exhale of inner exhaustion, "The day that he was given the title of being the best game leader in history."

My vision falls towards my left shoe, where I find that I am nearly standing on one of the explosives. The flashing timer now reads 01:09. Before I am given a chance to warn the others, a loud pop sails through the air. My eyes squint in the direction that the cloud came from earlier to see a gigantic wave of debris and sand shooting in a vertical angle.

My bottom lip falls slightly as I gently touch Austin's right shoulder, "Come on. We have to go, now!"

I do not wait around for a possible argument to take place. The toes of my shoes dig into the unstable foundation the best they can, propelling me to the right of the capsule.

The harsh intakes of air coming from behind, sends a shot of relief through the center of my chest knowing that they are not too far away.

My focus stays pinned on a small wall of sand that is now only ten-feet away from my current location.

A smile breaks against my face as I bring my feet to a sudden stall, "Look at this! Now, we have at least some form of shelter until it passes."

An uncontrollable, sarcastic laugh falls against my next phrase, "I bet, neither one of you would have thought of this, right?"

Without giving them a chance to express themselves, I speak again, "That is what I thought. I might be out of the running for the best game leader, but I am sure to win the best player. Look at this plan, it was beyond brilliant."

Emily tilts her head to the right, "Is there really an award for the best player?"

I wave my right arm in a careless manner towards her, "No, but it is going to be the first thing the Elders hear about when I get out of here."

Her attention is shifted off of me and onto the line of explosives that are being set off like a firework show in the distance.

Each spark of destruction ignites the atmosphere into a bundle of orange hues and freshly born, smokey clouds.

The silence between us has gone on for so long, the air is starting to become tense from being stagnant.

I forcibly clear my throat with one cough, "So, did Master Brutus give you guys a gift for this world? I think I somehow missed it, if he did."

Emily does not unlatch her eyes from the wall of debris being scattered throughout the area, "No."

I scuff at the fact that he forgot to do such an important part in the game.

An explosion that goes off roughly fifty-feet ahead causes us to drop to the ground behind the wall, hoping that it takes a majority of the impact.

Thankfully, it does. The soil beneath us shakes as soot rains down.

I tip my head back slightly to see a small note floating towards me.

My right, open palm extends in a vertical strike, snatching it out of the air.

My fingers run against the still burning edges as my eyes scan the ink embedded into the flesh,
'You are the gift, Arlenm. Make sure they use you wisely. Like always, I wish you the best of luck.
-MB'

The piece of paper takes no time at all to turn into ash, crumbling through the spaces of my fingers.

I watch as some of the particles swirl into a tornado-like formation in the distance before dancing up towards the sky.

Emily causes my breath to become lodged inside of my throat as she places her hand against my shoulder, "What did the note say?"

I attempt to relax my jumpy form by inhaling a deep breath,

"Congratulations, I am your gift. Feel free to use me as you need and from what I just saw, you are going to need me a lot."

The sly smirk resting high on the right side of my face is shattered as a closer explosion sends debris showering down on top of us.

I shake my head, hoping to clear off any sand from my form, but all it does is leave my head to clutter along my lap.

Emily's voice painfully scrapes against my mind, "Okay, we need you to help us get out of here before we are all killed."

CHAPTER FORTY-THREE:

The harsh vibration of my tone rings through the space, "I think our safest bet is to stay here until the explosives start to go off far enough away to our right."

Emily exhales loudly, the frustration rolls off of her tongue in my direction, "Oh, yeah. You are so helpful."

Austin glances in her direction, slowly shaking his head.

Her face melts into a small puddle of guilt, "I am sorry, Arlenm. I just really want to get home already."

The right side of my face twitches upwards, "Do you always want to leave the party early?"

She crosses her arms firmly over her chest, "This is not funny. I do not know why you both think it is."

My attention drifts towards Austin, who is staring at her annoyance with a growing smile.

A slight chuckle barrels up the back of my throat at the sight, "You can make any situation enjoyable. All you have to do is learn to stand under your own judgement."

Letters spew around me from her bottom lip, "This is really hard. I honestly do not understand how Austin is handling this all so well. I mean, come on, out of all people, this is Austin we are talking about. I do not understand why this whole being myself thing is so hard for me to grasp."

Austin speaks in a soothing manner, "It is not that the task itself is hard for you to grasp, you understand what you have to do. You are just not applying it to your life in the proper ways. You are not seeing results because you are still being blinded by limitations. Even though you are seeing growth in me, you do not want to admit it out of fear of being or remaining stuck where you are. If the situation was reversed and you head me say that same thing about you, hearing it from the current place you are at. You would take it personal and probably be very hurt and upset because of me.

However, at the point I am in with my journey. I know that this has nothing to do with me at all. I just happened to be here when you needed a way to let out some of your pain.

You have to stop thinking that lessons are a negative thing. You will never awaken to a day without tests and learning, but there will come a morning that you rise, ready to face them.

Either way a situation is going to occur, you will not be completely free from this physical law. However, you can walk through it or be dragged. If you walk, you are in control. That is where you want to be. Do not let someone else drag you forward. Trust me, it hurts a whole lot more."

I feel the motion of my vision roll up slightly, "All you have to do is never lose yourself in a world that is more confused than you. Use your stubbornness to refuse the negative, not to restrict the good."

A brief moment of silence falls around us. The tension is broken by shattering metal in the distance.

My voice collides with the echo of the gigantic burst, "Come on, we need to get going. We are heading towards the city."

Emily's eyes widen, "Do you think the portal is somewhere in there?"

I feel my head shake nervously, "I do not know. I do not think that is our main focus anymore. Master Brutus is known for building puzzles into the games. The only way to get access to the last portal is by figuring out what his plan is."

Austin keeps a calm stride to my right, "How do we figure that out?"

I attempt to quench my dry throat by swallowing roughly, "Maybe, I can find one of the other Mist-Formers and ask them for some information. There has to be someone in this game that is still loyal to me."

Emily shoots her attention sharply towards me, "What happens if we do not find someone?"

A dull pain scrapes against the left side of my chest under her doubt in my authority.

My right hand automatically raises towards the area. Upon impact a small crackle floods my ears.

I immediately put my attention onto the hidden pocket that lines the inside of my jacket. My fingers graze against the warm flesh of the paper. I retrieve the coffee-stained letter, carefully unfolding the unknown information that I so desperately crave to know.

The reflective surface of my eyes reveals the following message:
'This world is currently asleep. In order to be freed from the world, you have to wake them up.

Your timeline for this level is either going to be the length of two possible outcomes.

When you wake them up or when they kill you.

During this task, it is important to find your own strength as individuals.

Take Austin for example, he is the groups' GPS. He is like a metal detector for positive and negative emotions. Use his gift to either detour or guide you in the right direction.'

I feel my hands automatically folding the piece of paper back up. I lift my head slightly to see that we are now standing on the edge of the city.

The glow of neon lights strung along the buildings cause our eyes to squint in response to the blinding aura of a light yellow.

Austin leans his weight towards me, "What is the paper for?"

A slow breath flies from my tongue, "It is from Brutus. I figured out the puzzle."

I am not able to express my feelings any further due to a loud bell being rung from somewhere in the maze of concrete.

I feel like the scene is changing with every blink I take. Hundreds of people are now mindlessly filling every inch of the sidewalk, crammed together tightly into vehicles and getting in large lines to enter hollow structures.

Austin pulls his interest off of the scenery and onto me, "What were you saying before?"

It takes my mind a minute to connect the question, "Right. Yes, of course. The puzzle. It sounds quite simple. All we have to do is wake up all of these people."

The weight of shock beings draining into Emily's bottom lip causing it to fall slightly, "This is going to take forever. How are we supposed to do this? What is the plan?"

Austin tries to add hope to the situation, "Well, we could start with one person to see how long it takes to complete the cycle and then base a larger scale plan off of that information."

I feel my face squint sharply, "How exactly are you going to approach people with this?"

Austin shrugs his shoulders, "I was just planning on sharing the lessons with them. We could not have been the only beings in existence to have struggled with these things. It is probably a lot more common than you think."

I feel a gentle brush against my left forearm, stealing my focus.

It is Emily, her face is littered with concern, "I thought that we were in your world?"

My mouth curls slightly at the ends, "No. Well, the capsule you found me in, that was part of my world. This part, this is yours."

Emily's eyes widen sharply, "You have got to be kidding me. He changed the world?"

A soft laugh cannot be restrained inside of my throat, "He can do anything that he wishes. He is the game leader."

She throws her hands forward allowing her palms to slam against her thighs, "We cannot go in there and do this. There are billions of people on Earth and they are going to think we are insane. Is that what he wants?"

The chambers of my lungs fill with a crisp, deep inhale of a distant pine lingering through the currents of the breeze, "At first, it did not make sense on why he made this last-minute change. Now, it does. He wants you to think you are insane."

Austin squints his eyes, but his tone remains carefree, "What do you mean? Why would he want to do that?"

My vision dances around the scenery as I attempt to sort out my response, "He wants to make you feel like everything you just learned is non-sense. He is hoping that enough people will react in a negative manner to this information, sending you into a spiral of doubt. This uncertainty in yourself will cause a lack of faith which is going to make it easy for the people on this plane to destroy you without a single physical touch."

Emily feels a line of pain beginning to fill her throat, making it difficult for the words to be able to escape, "This is going to be freaking impossible. I am already going through so much the way it is. I cannot go out there like this. I am not ready. I do not think that I will make it to the end if I do."

My eyebrows move in an upwards motion to the tone of her voice, "The only person that you are fighting right now is yourself. If you cannot even convince yourself that this is in fact the best thing, you are never going to be able to help any of those people in there. You are really making this a lot harder than it has to be.

Emily, right in this moment, the only thing standing between you and getting out of this game is you. If you want to walk out of the hotel, you are going to have to walk through this world."

Her voice shakes as my firm tone is still echoing through her mind, "What if they are all like me? What if they cannot hear the messages that we are trying to relay to them? You heard the Captain yourself, Austin. We cannot force someone to understand information that they are not ready to."

Not a single word is stolen from his mind as he stares off into the city lights.

Emily throws her hands in my direction, "I think our GPS is broken."

I find my mind stumbling over itself as it tries to offer up soothing response.

Before I am given a fair chance to come up with any sort of answer for her rage, Austin's tone breaks against the air, "I know what we have to do to get out of here."

My eyes drift towards Austin sharply, "Is it attainable?"

Emily does not show any signs of relaxation under his claim to have found a solution. She remains held in a tense placement with her arms crossed tightly along her chest.

It does not take long for my attention to shoot towards Austin's voice that is now dripping into the silence, "It could be, yes. However, it is still going to become a large project no matter how we try to break it down. I think our best bet is to start with the highest vibrations on this plane and then work our way down."

Emily can feel her vision automatically squint under the idea, "Why would we start at the top? Why not start at the bottom with the people who need it the most?"

A long, slow breath grazes against the surface of his parted lips, "This is the best thing for the people on the lower levels.

Think about it, Emily is right. We can talk to people all day that are on a lower level and never get through to them. How is that doing them or us any good?

All we would be doing is going around like crazy people handing out all of this information of which they will not be able to apply to their lives. In order for them to be able to hear us, without any sort of muck, we have to raise their vibration for them until they are able to stand on their own once again."

Emily can feel her eyes dart towards me, "How are we supposed to do that?"

A slight smile breaks against the right side of his mouth, "If we help the higher levels open themselves up to even higher frequencies, it will naturally cause the lower levels to shift in an upwards movement as well. Therefore, by time we reach the *lowest* level there is on this plane, it will have been naturally lifting itself this entire time. So, that way when we are ready to help them, they will be able to hear us."

His words begin to play throughout my mind on repeat, "How will we know when we have successfully completed a level and how many different tiers are there?"

Austin nods slowly trying to give himself more time for a solution to roll in, "We can ask our guides to send us a consistent sign to let us know if there is more or not. We can even ask them how many levels we will be dealing with during this journey."

Emily exhales slowly, "Does that not kind of seem like we are cutting corners of the game?"

Austin shakes his head at a fast pace, "We would be out of our minds not to use their help. This is going to be a huge project."

Words begin flowing from my mouth without a filter, "What is the first sign that we are going to ask for?"

Austin stares up towards the flashes of light in the skyline, "We should probably figure out how many levels we are going to be dealing with. Once we know that, then we can ask how many people are in the sections or at least some general idea. That way, we can divide the work between us."

A blanket of silence begins to cover the air as I dig the toe of my right shoe further into the sand. I find it rather relaxing to watch the wind come through and brush it away.

My mindless entertainment is brought to a stall as Austin's voice comes to life, "Guides, please send me a sign of how many levels we are going to have to go through in order to gain freedom from this world."

He closes his eyes briefly as he whispers, "Thank you."

Emily can still feel small sparks of anxiety trying to gain control of her form, "What do we do now? Should we start looking for the signs?"

Austin shakes his head twice in a slow, controlled manner, "No. That is how confusion occurs. Just sit back, relax and the signs will come to us at the right time."

My chest pushes a breath of boredom from my parted lips, "So, what are we going to do while we wait?"

Austin's eyes begin to drop slightly, "I am exhausted. I am thinking about just laying down for a while and letting the guides work their magic. I am certain an answer will be brought to our attention by then."

Emily's shoulders slouch under hearing this plan, "I do not think I can sleep. I am on edge with all of the energy that is going on around us. Now, I am kind of getting excited for this sign to appear as well."

A small chuckle is released from his throat, "You do realize that they speak to us the most in our dreams, right?"

A fast shot of letters leaves her mind, "Fine."

Austin cannot remove the smirk from his mouth as he glances in my direction. By the look in his vision, I can tell that he is hoping I, too am enjoying the currently high vibration that is surrounding us.

I return a falsified grin, not wanting him to know that Emily is not the only one that is having a difficult time fully transforming.

Thankfully, it does not appear that he is picking up on my inner emotions as he puts his full attention onto getting comfortable upon the shifting grains of sand.

It does not take much convincing for mine and Emily's heavy, upper lids to remain sealed.

CHAPTER FORTY-FOUR:

Austin's eyes begin to flutter, his vision becomes lost in the still darkened sky that informs his sleeping mind that he has hardly received any rest at all.

The thoughts rumbling around inside of his mind become shattered as his focus is now pinned against the black void above.

While he lays still as a board, he sees that nine stars are stationed in his sight. The rest of the atmosphere seems dull in comparison.

He shoots the upper-half of his form into an excited, vertical placement.

A thought zooms against his brain receptors, *'There must be nine levels.'*

He throws his head to the left then towards the right in a quick motion, *'I do not want to wake them up, they seem to be resting peacefully. I would hate to be a disturbance, but the excitement is difficult to contain.'*

Austin inhales a large gulp of air, staring off, over the horizon awaiting the arrival of the sun.

He remains in that state of contentment until the first few rays of pink and purple illuminate a line of scattered clouds in the distance.

His eyes glow with sheer bliss as he watches the Divine, paint a fresh image for the beautiful day that lays ahead.

A shiver runs through the center of his chest, seeing that an orange shaded cloud rests in perfect formation, directly in his line of vision.

He is only able to examine the triangle briefly before the wind starts to wash it away.

It does not take long for his mind to start dissecting the new pieces of the puzzle.

My face squishes together tightly, feeling the warmth of the sun gliding against the right side of my face.

It does not take long for my ears to start to burn with the morning grog of Emily's tone, "Did you get any information?"

A slight smirk pulls against the left side of my face at the sight of her messy, blonde strands.

Austin speaks in a calm, uplifting demeanor, "Yes. I have more structure for the plan."

Emily beams with delight under the information, "Great! What did you all get?"

He nods his head once in confirmation to her excitement, "So, there are nine levels of vibration, that we have to pass through and alter in order to be given a chance at finding the portal. The structure is set up sort of like a triangle. At the very top, in the highest vibration rests a smaller group of people. From there on out, the vibration lowers and the occupancy grows larger. I have yet to get an estimate of exactly what we are going to be dealing with number wise, but at least we have a good idea of where we are going."

Emily forces the smile to remain against her lips as her

internal frequency begins to be drained of all hope that she held only moments ago, "This is going to take us forever! There has to be a faster way to do this."

A fast shift in the energy that surrounds us occurs, twisting the high vibration that I felt only moments ago and manipulating the situation to prevent me from being able to breathe in peace.

I do not become surprised to hear a yawn slip past my lips, the humidity in the air covers the surface of my tongue.

My head shakes slightly in irritation, "It does not really matter how fast we accomplish it. Time is not our enemy in this world. We need to focus on the parts of the world that are going to be a potential obstacle now, so we can come up with a plan to stop it before they stop us."

Austin allows my words to consume him, "He is right. We need to walk into this prepared. We do not know how any of these people are going to react when we start approaching them with the topic regardless, if we they in a higher vibration or not. We need to figure out a way to remain calm and sturdy."

Emily releases a choppy breath from her tightened lips in hopes of soothing her inner discomfort with the situation, "We have to remain non-violent."

Austin extends his right, open palm out towards her in an act of comfort, "Not to worry. We are not going to be fighting anyone. We have no reason to worry about that. The training that we endured in the last world will help our emotions remain under our control during the tasks. I am telling you, I have been thinking about this all night. I was not able to get a lot of sleep, so my mind did what it does best. It wanders. I have weighed out the different ways that we could be aided in the situation. We now know for sure that when we ask for answers from our guides that we are given them. Specific answers, that come with just enough information. So, I wanted to figure out what the next thing we need to ask for is. Unfortunately, there is only one thing that I think we are lacking in this current moment."

He is unable to finish giving the rest of this theory because my uncontrollable tongue begins to release a question, "What is it that we need? Do you think that they will provide us with it?"

Emily slows the pace of her breathing to a slow crawl, not wanting to miss a word he speaks, "We need people, but not just any people. We need someone who has been through the darkness and walked out with the light burning within."

My mind starts hitting the obstacle between the two sides of my brain, "Okay, so this is easy enough to fix. If they are unable to send us physical aid. We can just gather up all of the people that we helped in the first level, explain to them the situation and hope that they agree. I really do not think we have many other options for that at this moment."

Austin runs the grooved pad of his right thumb against his bottom lip, "I can ask as well. It will not hurt anything, the worst thing that would happen is that our request is denied. Is there anything else that we need them to manifest before we attempt to head forward?"

My right foot taps in an out of rhythm melody, "They are not going to be able to just make people magically appear out of thin air, that meets these requirements. It is impossible."

A familiar, female voice echoes through the morning air, "You are right. That is why we are here."

▼ ▼ ▼

The Captain steps forward, giving me relief to the last question that was so carelessly thrown from my lips, "When I started this game, my soul was broken into six different pieces. These parts where consumed with both love and fear, hidden under the false masks of who I thought I had to be. Who the world of earth told me that I had to become to be strong, confident, loving of self and others.

When my spiritual ascending began, I was introduced to you, Arlenm. You were relentless. Every time I fell down, you only found pleasure in my fear. The same fear, I only believed was true my whole life because that was what you told me I deserved."

My eyes twitch and tense sharply under hearing this injustice towards my image.

I begin to walk out of anger towards the Captain, my right hand is thrown back above my head, being directed towards her physical form with the intention of nothing but destruction.

I look into her eyes to try and find a glimpse of fear before releasing all of my frustration out onto her.

My right shoulder relaxes so greatly, my arm can no longer be held in the air, it drops towards my thigh twice before coming to a crawl.

The weight of my head falls to the right, "Why do you have no fear of me? Why aren't you scared? How can you smile while being held under my power?"

The Captain releases a soft melody of laughter to surround my form, "When we first started this adventure together, I was afraid. I felt so much fear, I could not get up off of the floor. Then I was graced with the pleasure of meeting you. At that time, my lessons were divided into six categories, each one different, but all fear is felt the same. It was easier to understand, heal, learn and grow from when the pieces were broken up."

Before my mouth is given a chance to sort a response, Austin appears on her right side.

The weight of my bottom lip drops slightly as I admire him. I have never seen him at such peace. The sight itself is irritating.

I am so consumed with my feelings, I cannot speak.

I feel helpless as I watch the Captain's lips move once more, "Austin, Raven, Luke, Emily, Nash and Morgan. Each one was being tormented by energies from me and you at the same time. Each one bears the first initial of their earth label or image from you, I am the part of them that does not need to be defined. When they started to learn, heal and grow throughout the game, they choose to follow the truth because it made them feel better in ways and on levels that even they never even believed were imaginable, yet here they all stand completely healed.

Their motivation towards a better existence for themselves and all others is what removed the illusions of fear you placed around them.

That is why you are now experiencing confusion, defeat, discomfort and fear."

Tears of uncertainty fall from my vision. I look down to regather myself.

The structure of my head pulls up slightly, all of the air is taken from my lungs at the sight of it now being just myself and the Captain.

My response to the occurrence is draped in despair, "Where did they go?"

A soft smile beams against me, "The energies that you gave to them have been healed and are now neutralizing with the universal energies. The energies that they received from me were kept, decoded, learned, accepted and applied to every detail of them and their lives. The growth, love and peace you saw in them, all was a result of this cleansing that occurred during the game."

I shake my head in irritation and disbelief as it drains from my lips, "Okay, but again, the answer remains unclear. Where did they go?"

She releases a slow breath of contentment, "They returned to me, so I could gain all of the experiences, knowledge, learning, healing and growth then combine it with all gained from the past. Once it is fully applied, I will gain more every single day. From now on, the biggest change is that I will only learn my lessons from love instead of fear, from source instead of man, from growth instead of destruction."

My knees fall weak as I feel I cannot accept the truth, "Are you complete now?"

She beams under the truth, "You will always be expanding, learning and healing. *'Complete'* implies an end, but there is no limit to knowledge, love, healing, growth and progress."

A tear falls from my vision, "I have no idea what I am going to do now. I have lost everything. Every detail of who I am feels completely meaningless to me in this moment, almost as if I have lost myself. All the work I have done for my entire existence, all the creations that I have made, for what? I cannot see things clearly for me in this moment or for my future. It all feels bleak without meaning, like nothing will ever be the same again. I do not know where I am needed or what my purpose is outside of destruction."

She steps closer to me in comfort, "Your work with me has and will always be important. You will always be needed by me."

Anger fuels my brows inward as I step back, "I don't work for you, I work for Master Brutus."

She nods once in understanding of my disapproval of her words, "Master Brutus is who you work for, you are correct, but you only work to better him. He is the outer influence that made you believe all of your actions, reactions, thoughts, gestures, words and emotions were weak, pathetic and wrong if they stemmed from a place of love, care, peace and understanding, unless you were like him. Although, it did not take long before you found out that even when you try your hardest to be like him, it will still never please him or make him respect you.

This happens to us all, everyone who comes to this physical plane loses our memory upon arrival. When you are first gaining your memory back, it is easy to be influenced by the fear that exists on the physical plane because at that point in your life, there is no other option provided other than the ones you see all the time. When you try to create something from love, difference, peace and happiness you are considered weak and mistreated for your actions, so like everyone else in the world, who tried to shine their light through the darkness around them, they were dimed and forced to surrender to things that they did not agree with or even want to do, simply because they thought that there was no other way. We believe this truth until we awaken and are introduced to our spiritual guides, the Divine and the truth. This is when you start to heal, when you work with me instead of against me."

I can barely be understood through my tears, "How are we connected so strongly? I do not understand, I only just met you here recently. How could you have been affecting me my entire existence?"

She inhales a deep breath of crisp air, one of my favorite feelings, "I have always been with you, suggesting, wishing to alter, change and recreate something new, something of love. You have not just met me. In fact, you saw glimpses of me coming through your actions, reactions, gestures, thoughts and emotions your entire life. At the time, you were just still trying to find a strong foundation of what was real, so I would go unnoticed or pushed off to the side because you felt my input was not helpful, only a potential to get more damaged.

Arlenm, I am the soul and you are my physical world imagination. You are what allows me to co-create my life alongside the creator. Your perceptions of yourself, me, the world, others, the Divine, etc. were just focused and set to be viewed through a lens of fear instead of processing everything through love."

My breath stops, "I am the one who destroyed you so deeply?"

Her consistency brings me deep peace, "Some was from you and some was from others. You taught me the results of what happens when you treat someone with fear and they taught me why it is done in the first place towards others, so I could understand all sides before deciding which path I want to use constantly. When you return to me and we become one again, all of my healing, growth and truth will naturally reset you to perceive all things from love and only love."

I step forward three strides before collapsing at her feet, onto my knees.

She drops her weight into the same placement.

Through my blurred eyes, I see nothing but the destruction I have caused, "How do we begin this reset? I'd like to do it as quickly as possible. I am ready for something better. I know I deserve peace, we all do."

She takes my hands inside of hers, peace washes over me and all worries vanish.

I can feel myself drifting into a deeper meditation to the sound of her voice, "Arlenm, I forgive you. You did not know. No one is upset with you, this happens to everyone on this plane. That is why we are here—to learn.

Do not be upset for the learning that brought you here. Do not feel guilt or remorse for any behavior that was applied from fear. We all have the same experiences, just different situations that teach them to us. That is why we see separation between our pain and theirs, but all emotion is felt the same.

More clarity will be brought to this area and many others, all you have to do is now forgive yourself. You are looking at this situation from a place of guilt, disappointment, pain, uncertainty and many more perceptions of fear. They are only causing you more unnecessary discomfort. In order to forgive yourself, you must look at the truth.

You got through things that you never dreamed you would have ever found answers to. Look at all the times you kept pushing through and never gave up, until the results you wanted appeared. In order to achieve that, you had to have trust with the Divine, divine realm, yourself, guides and spiritual family and animals, who are always guiding you to be able to find this knowledge that sets you free from all fear you held. Alrenm, your actions are not what destroyed you, they are what lead you here, to this moment of growth."

A deep breath intertwines with my lungs as I sink deeper into peace. I can feel my energy merging with her and only one thought consumes me with joy, 'I cannot wait to go home to love, healing and the truth. I always knew I'd find the place I belonged and longed for my entire existence on this plane. It is actually a relief, to know this place was within and around me the entire time. I was always safe. I was always loved.'

I stand, staring into the orange sky, mixing with swirls of pink, behind some unnamed canyons in the distance, 'Once I ascended, I knew I could not write the eighth novel. I lived the Land of ARLENM series as I wrote it, only then learning about this after living the eighth book myself.

Once you are connected with your spiritual guides, you will find all the same, just in your own way and on your own pace. If I wrote book eight, you'd be influenced by my creations and expansion. You came here to build your own with no influence from a human, only your spiritual guides and the truth they teach you.

We are all unlimited and what we create from this point in our journeys, should be just as individual as all creations were made to be in their own ways.

Thank you for your patience and understanding.
Thank you for healing.
Thank you for being here.

Until we meet again.

-Sam (:

ABOUT THE AUTHOR

Previous works include:

Man of the House – Murder Mystery
Madison's Christmas – Children's Story
Land of ARLENM Vol 1-6 – Self-
Help/Fantasy
The Portal – Real Paranormal
Between the Pages – Romance

More books to come soon! For latest releases go to vibrations-of-love.company.site